SHADOW'S FORCE

SHADOW ISLAND SERIES: BOOK FOUR

MARY STONE
LORI RHODES

Created with Vellum

This book is dedicated to those who lost loved ones in a deadly storm.

DESCRIPTION

Which is more dangerous...Mother or Human Nature?

Twelve hours earlier, Interim Sheriff Rebecca West was enjoying a casual lunchtime burger. Now she's preparing for a hurricane headed straight for Shadow Island. While hauling sandbags and calming town officials, the last thing she needs is a stunned man stumbling into the sheriff's department.

Covered in blood.

Clearly in shock, the man doesn't know who he is and only mutters about needing help finding a mermaid. Is he distraught because he killed someone or because he witnessed a horrific event?

Rebecca needs to find out—and fast.

Fighting the torrential rain and wind, Rebecca discovers the victim, posed and decorated like a mermaid. Is the catatonic man the killer? Or is something more sinister at work?

With very little support, she has to work quickly before the island is completely cut off from the mainland and any evidence is destroyed by the natural disaster. It's all hands on deck as Rebecca and the entire department scramble to prepare for a hurricane...and solve a murder.

From its enigmatic beginning to the nail-biting conclusion, Shadow's Force—the fourth book in the Shadow Island Series by Mary Stone and Lori Rhodes—will make you fear the storms of nature and love.

1

Rain covered the town like gray gauze, making everything blurry and muted.

It was a dark and stormy night...

He scoffed at the idea of such an overused line being used in connection with him. Nothing in his entire damn life had ever been dramatic enough to be part of some epic story. Sure, his had always been good...safe. Stable job, nice house, and a woman who loved him. The ideal for 'most anyone. Most people would think he'd had it all.

Emphasis on *had.*

He rushed to unlock the door of the Maserati he'd been so proud of, not caring that his blood-soaked hands would mar its pristine finish. Slippery fingers struggling to grip the key fob, he glanced over his shoulder toward the house.

Her house.

He looked away.

With the car finally unlocked, he ducked into its protective shell to escape the swirling winds and sheets of pounding rain. He struggled against the powerful gusts to pull the driver's door closed. Peering through the downpour, the outline of her home was barely visible. Heart threatening to break his ribs, he flipped on the windshield wipers and backed out of the driveway.

Cranked to the highest setting, the wipers struggled to fight back the storm's assault. The Italian luxury car's powerful LED headlights strained against the onslaught to illuminate the road. Worried about the rapidly deteriorating conditions, he attempted to switch on the lane assist feature the salesman had spent more than fifteen minutes touting. It wouldn't activate.

Right. Low visibility rendered it inoperable. What the hell was it even good for, then?

Against common sense, he pressed the accelerator, his gut screaming to get away. He had to tell someone what he'd seen.

What I've done.

The car dinged, angry that he hadn't yet buckled his seat belt. As he rounded the bend at the end of the road, he reached for the strap. The car drifted. Panic surged as he gripped the steering wheel again, his crimson hands slipping over the leather as he desperately attempted to correct the spin.

Steer into the slide.

The words from his driver's education class so many years ago whispered through his mind. His slick hands knew what to do, rapidly switching places, until the fishtail straightened out.

Relief washed over him, and he craned his head in a small circle, unknotting the muscles in his shoulders and neck.

What have I done? How am I going to explain?

There would be time for those thoughts later. First, he had to—

A downed tree appeared through the haze, sprawled

across the road, and his candy-apple red car slammed into the thick trunk before he could react or even blink.

Bang!

The airbag exploded, punching him harder than Mike Tyson's fist as it stopped his unbuckled body from its forward pursuit. His head snapped back and...

MINUTES OR HOURS LATER, he blinked awake and immediately wished he hadn't. Pain was everywhere. His neck, his ribs, his arms. Even his face pulsed with every heartbeat.

Where am I? And how did I get here?

His knees screamed as he moved his legs away from the collapsed dash. He'd been in a crash, that much was clear. And was that gas he smelled?

I need to get out of here.

Swatting the nylon of the airbag out of his way, his hand came down on a different type of material. Plastic. Upon closer inspection, he realized it was a poncho left in the car for times such as these. Based on the sound of rain pounding the roof of the vehicle, he'd need it.

Groaning against the movements of his arms, he pulled the poncho over his head before attempting to open the door. It was stuck. When he muscled it with a forceful nudge of his shoulder, it finally opened, and he spilled out onto the street, his knees coming down into a lake of water.

Using the door for leverage, he hauled himself to his feet and began to walk toward a halo of red-and-white light about a football field away.

Must find help.

The thought slowed his pace. Sure, he was in pain, but for some reason, he didn't think the help he needed was for him.

For who, then?

Pressing his hands into the sides of his throbbing head, he tried to think. Where was he? Why was he here? Where had he been going? And who needed help?

I'm supposed to find something...but what? Why can't I remember?

A gust of wind tore at the plastic poncho, exposing his face to the pelting rain, and he pulled its hood farther down to protect his skin. A fast, turbulent flow raced for the street grate below him, where fresh green leaves choked the torrent.

Why was he out in this storm?

Try as he might, he couldn't remember.

Nothing looked familiar.

His foot slipped in the running water, shooting out from underneath him. He nearly went to his knees again but managed to stay upright. Barely.

"Where did all this water come from?"

There was no answer to his question. The roads were abandoned. In fact, it seemed the entire world had been abandoned. There was no sign of life anywhere.

He tried to shake his head like a Labrador fresh out of a pond, desperate to stop the rain from its relentless attack. Pain rocked his head at the movement, and he held out both hands for balance as the world spun around him.

Easy.

When the world stopped turning, he focused on the red-and-white blinking lights again. Only half a football field away now, if his depth perception was intact.

He bent at the waist into the wind, keeping his head down so he could see. Rain came down so hard it assaulted him from every direction, above and below, as it splashed back up into his face. Everything was black, white, or gray except for the flashing lights, which blended into an pinkish blur, painting the world in a dizzying spiral.

"There."

The swirling lights brought fresh pain, and he shielded his eyes from the invasion.

Hunched over against the rain, he moved toward the flashing lights with his hand raised like a blinder. Thick crimson lined his fingernails despite the rain washing over them. He recognized it now. Blood.

Mine?

He didn't know.

A deep male voice shouted words he couldn't make out. Shapes of people ran in and out of a building. Like a moth to a flame, he was drawn to the strobing lights causing his brain such distress.

Bile rose in his throat and he choked it back down.

"Help!"

He stumbled forward, buffeted by the wind shrieking around him like the souls of the damned. Hot liquid ran down his face, and, with shaking hands, he reached up to touch his cheeks. Tears. Why was he crying?

It didn't matter. All that mattered was reaching those lights. The cry that came from his mouth scared him. It was so weak and sad he didn't recognize it as his own. *Keep moving.* Help was close now. And he needed that desperately.

A sob jumped up from his chest. "Help!"

No one could hear him.

Maybe the shrieking he'd heard was that of his own wretched soul. Or death reaching out to take him too.

Should he give in to the death that felt like it had been chasing him? Was that what called him to the building? His legs moved him closer to his destiny.

The statue of a woman with a fish tail illuminated in

flashes of red and white. A mermaid. He recoiled at her presence.

How? How was she here?

She stood between him and his destination. It was a sign. The mermaid pointed at a nearby door, as if she wanted him to follow.

Did salvation wait on the other side?

Redemption?

Damnation?

It didn't matter. He had to go through. That much he knew.

After fighting the door, he shuffled into a room bustling with people. Blue uniforms raced around gray ones. Raincoats lined an entire wall as people walked through the lobby.

He started to shrug off his poncho, but his arms were too tired to bother. Staggering forward, he rested his hands on the counter. A puddle with pink ribbons formed around each of them.

Little ponds of blood. Revulsion filled him, and he tried to yank his arms back, but he couldn't move.

Am I dying?

On the other side of the desk, a Black woman was talking into a microphone attached over her ear, her head lowered as she scribbled notes. "I'll have someone right over. Just sit tight and try to stay calm." She pressed a button and lifted her head. "Can I help—" Her dark eyes widened in horror.

That same horror was taking over his insides.

"Help." The word barely escaped his throat.

She jumped to her feet. "Sir? Are you all right? What happened?" Her voice was so kind, so concerned. She seemed so caring.

He reached out to her but stopped. Blood dripped down his fingers, dropping onto her desk.

He looked down at his chest. Through the clear poncho, he could see his blood-soaked shirt. Had he been stabbed? Was that why he'd been in the rain to begin with?

His mind beat at his skull as if trying to break free. But it couldn't. Pain stabbed him like a knife being driven into each eyeball. There was something he had to do. It was why he had come here. He knew that now.

"Darian! Greg! Get up here!"

The screaming woman frightened him, and he took half a step back. His shoe squished, and he stared down at the drenched and worn carpet. There was blood in thick, overlapping circles on his pants. Would he ever be clean again?

"I...help. I... Some...I think."

Screams echoed in his head.

The woman's lips were pursed together. It wasn't her screaming. Slowly surveying the room, he found every eye on him. No one was screaming. The screams were in his head.

Screams and hammers.

Tears welled up and rained down his cheeks, mixing with the blood at his feet.

"I think I hurt someone."

2

Just yesterday, Interim Sheriff Rebecca West had been sitting in a cozy little café eating a juicy hamburger and enjoying a few moments of respite. Now, at the ungodly hour of three thirty in the morning, here she was, soaked to the bone and flinging sandbags.

With a grunt, Rebecca heaved the next burlap bag of sand. Her senior deputy, Hoyt Frost, was much better at getting the damp sand into the bags, so she was on stacking duty. Which was not something she had thought would be in her job description as sheriff.

Interim Sheriff, she reminded herself.

"It's weird, though. Of course, the tourists would have you believe it only rains when they're here."

All up and down the line, voices called out from the haze of salty fog. Rebecca wasn't even sure if this was true fog or spray from the ocean reaching their location.

Someone scoffed. "True! Do you remember three years ago when that tropical storm was supposed to die out before it hit us? Totally ruined my midweek plans."

"Yup, we didn't even bother getting extra gas for the generator that time."

"Got caught with my sump pump down too!"

"That sounds like a personal problem there." Rebecca directed her response to the line in general, unsure of who had said that last bit.

She wanted to ask why a sump pump on this tiny island was even needed but knew she'd get laughed at for tossing out the question. She'd only heard of sump pumps being used in homes with basements. Surely there were no basements on this tiny island. They were only a few feet above sea level, after all.

Instead of forming the question, she listened to the peals of laughter, echoing strangely in the thick, cold air. It was amazing that these people could chat and joke while preparing for a hurricane to wreak havoc on their community.

Like apparitions, they stepped out of the mist, materializing just a few feet away from her. Until they were right on top of her, she couldn't make out any features as the lights around them swirled.

And Hoyt said this isn't even as bad as it's going to get. Why can't we just evacuate like sane people?

Since hearing the ominous forecast over lunch yesterday, Rebecca had spent most of her time poring through the emergency preparedness manual. There was a ton of information to absorb, with details about evacuation procedures, distribution of backup radios, issuing alerts, and on and on. She hated that there hadn't been enough time to soak in all the policies within the massive binder. Hopefully, her crew would help fill in the gaps.

Her phone vibrated in her pocket, and she assumed it was another one of the hundreds of alerts she'd received over the past few hours. Viviane or one of the guys would radio if they needed her. If desperate, they would use her pager. Her phone would have to wait.

Sunrise was still hours away—not that she thought they'd be able to see by then. For now, no more than the palest of gray light waxed and waned with the gusts off the ocean.

Monday morning was supposed to bring a very different type of storm into Rebecca's life in the form of a nine o'clock meeting that would determine her fate as the island's sheriff. Viviane Darby, her friend and the department's dispatcher, had filled her in on Shadow Island's unique charter.

Unsurprisingly, Richmond Vale, an asshat of royal order, had managed to add a clause giving the Select Board—*his* name for what normal towns called their county commission —the freedom to control the hiring and firing of the sheriff between formal elections. Rebecca had learned all about that after Albert Gilroy, an equally royal asshat, had threatened her job during her last case.

As chairman of that board, Vale wielded vast control over Shadow Island. What he didn't wield control over? The weather.

With a hurricane barreling toward them, that meeting had been postponed. Her *interim* label would have to endure a bit longer.

Not that she was worried. Once Albert Gilroy—an influential islander whose son was killed not long ago—pulled his secret candidate, no one else had stepped up for consideration. The only person on the island with enough experience to fill the role was Deputy Frost, and he'd made it clear to everyone not to dare ask. That left Rebecca as the only choice.

If she even wanted the job.

This career path wasn't one Rebecca had envisioned when she arrived on Shadow Island for some much-needed R&R a few weeks ago. After confronting the people behind her parents' murders and taking a bullet for her trouble, she'd just wanted to spend a few months on the same island where she'd vacationed with her parents when she was a child.

She could clear her head, shake loose some demons, and plot her future.

Fate had other plans. Before she'd barely unpacked her first box, Sheriff Alden Wallace had approached her, asking for help. Short-staffed, he'd needed her assistance when a teenage girl went missing. When Wallace had been killed in an ambush, Rebecca had been forced into the interim role. She'd tried to walk away from the job and its responsibilities more than once, only to be pulled back in each time.

And now, here she stood, shoulder to shoulder with the people of the island, of *her* island, trying to stave off disaster as a Category 2 hurricane turned their way. When Mother Nature decided to change plans, all a person could do was scramble and hope to keep up with her.

Inhaling deeply, Rebecca regretted the need for air when she was assaulted by a new wave of seaweed, rotting wood, and something else she couldn't name. The scents of a heavy storm over the sea shrouded the island with a warning of imminent doom.

Or maybe it was the vaguely surreal atmosphere of everything.

Colors were muted or wholly wiped away. The shrieks of the wind kept messing with her hearing. Her nose was stuffed with the salted moldering of tidewrack that had washed ashore. Thanks to the shifting grayness, she had no sense of time. The squalls pressed her raincoat against her, making it difficult to move even as the blasts of water trickled in under her hood and down her back and chest.

Her new HiVis reflective slicker with *Sheriff* blazoned across the back trapped her body heat while sweat droplets battled the rain in a contest of which could make her more miserable. Hoyt had gifted her the raincoat, and it even fit. Her senior deputy—or more likely his wife Angie—must have special-ordered it. From experience, she knew nothing in the storeroom was her size. Even the makeshift utility belt her senior deputy's wife had cobbled together for her was too big for her slender frame.

The jacket may have been too good at keeping her warm but not so good at keeping her dry. The rain was finding every possible path inside its protective outer shell.

I'm humid. And sticky. Wrapped in plastic. At the same time, I'm slowly losing my fingertips with every sand-covered bag.

Rebecca picked up the next bag to sling when a voice from behind distracted her.

"I thought this one was going to blow himself out on Florida and leave us alone."

"Got too far north before he started turning. Now he's not even going to touch South Carolina from the looks of things. He's going to bring it all to us."

More folks added to the good-natured banter as the islanders took the news in stride. Judging by some of the younger voices mixed in, the volunteers consisted of anyone strong enough to lift a bag or shovel.

"Looks like Boris likes us more."

"Well, I don't like Hurricane Boris." Rebecca dropped her load on the barrier that was already four high and two deep. She shifted to her right to start the next section after rubbing her shoulder. "Dammit! The falling barometric pressure is making me feel twice my age. I thought only my grandma had sore joints when a storm rolled in."

A man laughed as his shape came into focus.

"Hang in there, ma'am. If you'd like, I can find someone younger to take your place." Hoyt's broad smile and tall frame appeared out of the mist. "If you're up to the task, just keep slinging the bags until you get to the curb on the other side. We have to do our best to keep this road from getting washed out. If we end up needing to evacuate, it's one of the main throughways."

That tracked with what the evacuation map indicated. Rebecca had nearly memorized the various routes, which increased her confidence in her ability to keep the people of Shadow Island as safe as possible.

Hoyt hadn't been to the office yet either, so he was wearing his personal rain gear. The bright reflective tape on her law enforcement gear acted like a lighthouse, cutting through the fog while he got to hide in the shadows.

"You've got a few years on me, Deputy. Is that why you've chosen to simply supervise tonight? Or, um, this morning?" Her ribbing of the senior deputy brought hearty laughter from the people working closest to Rebecca.

Hoyt laughed and patted her on the back. He held up a plastic-sheathed map of the town in front of her face so she could see it. Blue, red, and purple lines were marked along different roads.

"You mentioned when you got here earlier that you'd reviewed the evacuation map. We keep one in every cruiser, so it's there in case you need to refer to it later. Same one we use for search parties. The purple line is the main route to the bridge. That's the line we absolutely have to protect. We're right here." He tapped an intersection.

Rebecca shouted her reply as another band of rain swept across the line. "What's the estimated landfall at this point?"

"Last report we got was about twelve hours." Hoyt's booming voice was muted in the raging winds.

Twelve hours?

"That's not enough time. I thought we'd be further along with our preparations."

Hoyt laughed. "That's Mother Nature for you. Unpredictable and prone to anger. Welcome to hurricane season!"

She'd always thought hurricane season was in the fall, not in June. Then again, she'd learned a great deal since coming to the island.

"How do you guys deal with this kind of shit?" Rebecca threw her hands up, indicating the muted mire encasing them. She tossed another bag onto the growing barrier.

"We don't." Someone on the stacking line called out, his voice tinged with that odd quaver from the constantly changing air pressure. "Storms this bad are rare, and most hit farther south and slow down before getting to us. Shadow hasn't had a direct hit in…uh. Hey, Larry, when was the last time we had a storm hit us first?"

Rebecca did a double take. Was this Larry the Handyman? The man, the myth, the legend? She'd only met him in passing, but she thought it was him.

An older man—his features fuzzy with the fog—responded. "Five years ago, toward the end of the season. Big one. Didn't use ta get the big ones in the spring. With warming sea temperatures, I 'spect this is going to become more common."

Rebecca groaned. "Fantastic."

Lights swept over them as a truck pulled up and stopped on the road.

A spattering of cheers rang out as people could momentarily see what they were doing. The joyous sound doubled as more bodies spilled out of the vehicle and joined them.

"We stacking or filling?"

"Fill!" The response rang out from several voices at once.

People shuffled into new roles, making room for the new arrivals. It seemed like at least half the town was turning out to help. Everyone seemed to know exactly what to do, as if it were a dance they all knew the steps for.

Except for Rebecca. At least not completely. Reading a binder wasn't the same as living through it. And while she hoped this would be her last hurricane, she knew the experience she was currently acquiring would pay dividends in the future.

A vibration tickled her leg, and she jerked, looking down. The manual had warned about downed power lines. When it happened again, she scolded herself for being jumpy. And stupid. It was just her phone. Again.

Rebecca recalled the lengthy chapter on what she'd dubbed "the care and feeding of your emergency radio." While most of the information was common sense, there had been a section on handing out additional two-way radios to as many emergency personnel as possible. Several more paragraphs were dedicated to the use of non-rechargeable batteries.

Having been called to the sandbag line before she'd finished reviewing all the materials, Rebecca hadn't had the opportunity to address the emergency communication system. She made a mental note to prioritize getting the radios distributed.

After just one more bag, her phone vibrated again. No. This vibration came from her waist and was accompanied by a shrill, piercing note. Her pager. That was a completely different matter. No one was going to page her unless it was an emergency.

She turned, stepping out of line so she wouldn't impede progress.

Another body took her place without a word. Muttering, she pulled her arm into her raincoat to tug the pager from her waistband. Still keeping it inside the plastic, she lifted to her face the small, square device that brought her back to the time of the dinosaurs, ducking 'til her chin was nearly on her chest so she could read the tiny screen. Pagers had been invented during the stone age, back before cell phones, but still worked for hospital staff where cell signals couldn't reach. And for island towns in the direct path of hurricanes.

The pager showed the station number, followed by 911—a little redundant, considering everything.

"What's going on?" Hoyt yelled over a sudden blast of hot wind.

Uh-oh, that wasn't good. A hot wind was always a bad omen when it came to tornadoes. Did that hold true for hurricanes? If the wind was blowing hot, did they even have twelve hours before the hurricane was on them?

"There's an emergency at the station."

He frowned and shook his head, flinging water that was lost in the heavy rainfall. "The whole island has an emergency, West."

"Har dee har."

He sighed dramatically. "I didn't get paged, so they only want you. Go on. We can handle this while you sit inside in your cushy new chair, sip lattes, and nibble on croissants."

Despite knowing he was joking, Rebecca felt guilty as she headed to the department-issued Explorer. It took a herculean effort to open the door against the squalls, and her shoulder let her know it was not appreciated. She fell into the driver's seat and pulled her legs in before the door slammed shut on its own.

Rebecca grabbed the radio, not even bothering with the phone jammed into her damp pants.

"West here. You paged? Over."

"Sheriff, we've got a weird one." Viviane Darby was the receptionist and daytime dispatcher at the station. She'd become a good friend to Rebecca in the short time they'd known each other. "A man walked in covered in blood but doesn't know why. It's caked into his cuticles, and he's even got some streaked through his hair. He also doesn't seem to know his name or where he came from. Over."

Yeah, that definitely sounded weird.

"Copy that. Could he have been in a car wreck? Over."

"He has some trauma to his face, but I wouldn't begin to guess how he got it. There wasn't a visible wound large enough to cause that amount of blood. And he had it all over him. It dripped all over the carpet in the lobby. I thought it was a practical joke at first. He was so slathered in it. He's in shock and doesn't know how the blood got there." There was a pause. "He said he thinks he hurt someone. Over."

"Hurt? Not killed? Over." Rebecca considered the implications. If someone was hurt, that was at least a silver lining to the horror of a man coated in blood. *Hurt* meant they could still be saved.

"Roger that. He said 'hurt,' but that's an awful lot of blood." Doubt filled every word. "Over."

Rebecca felt that silver lining tarnishing. "So we have someone out there who has lost a lot of blood and our only witness doesn't know where or who they are? Over."

"Yeah, pretty much...oops. Over."

Rebecca smiled at the dispatcher's lapse in using the official jargon when on the radio.

"Anything else? Over."

"Actually, yes. Can you remind me later to congratulate Melody on her excellent vacation-timing skills? Over."

Rebecca smiled. Their night-shift dispatcher had certainly picked a good time to be off the island. "Will do. Over and out."

Staring out the windshield, Rebecca could only see the two cars parked adjacent to the SUV. Visibility was nonexistent. And she needed to brave these conditions and attempt to find an injured person, hopefully before they died.

If they hadn't already.

3

Turning into the slide, Rebecca eased her foot off the brake as the SUV hydroplaned past the sheriff's station parking lot. She just missed sideswiping the emergency vehicles parked along the road.

The paramedic, standing next to his ambulance, watched as she maneuvered the vehicle. Once she regained control, he gave her a nod, then climbed into the back of his truck and closed the door behind him.

Blowing out a breath that fogged up the windshield even more, Rebecca put the vehicle in reverse and backed into the parking lot. She was partially reassured by the paramedic's calm demeanor, but she needed to question the bloody man and get as many answers as she could.

Watching the direction the wind blew the rain in front of the streetlamp, she waited until she wouldn't have to fight against it. Once it shifted, she pushed open the door and jumped out. She splashed down into a puddle, but the entire town was a puddle at this point. Keeping her head down, she ran as fast as the storm would permit for the door.

She slipped into the building and threw her hood back.

The loud thrum of a Shop-Vac whirring near the door welcomed her.

"Careful." Between the rain hitting the glass and the motor of the vacuum, Greg Abner had to yell to be heard. "I'm trying to suck up as much of the rain and bloody mess as I can." He pulled the door shut with one tanned hand. In the other, he held the black hose of an industrial vacuum. A bucket at his side brimmed with brownish-pink water.

Rebecca stared at the bucket. "It was that bad?"

He shrugged, turning his brown eyes back to the disgustingly squishy carpet. "Not the worst I've seen, but the rain made it drip everywhere. The guy managed to get blood on almost everything before we could get him to the back."

"Including my desk." Viviane had a spray bottle and paper towels in her gloved hands. She flipped her shoulder-length black hair over her shoulder and narrowed dark eyes at the desk as if it were a crouching spider.

"We got some samples collected, but then we had to clean it up. It was a biohazard." Greg flipped off the machine and pried off the lid so he could empty it. At sixty-one years old, though he'd been working more than usual since her arrival, the deputy was officially a part-timer.

"Tell me what happened." Rebecca pondered the soaked carpet and wondered why anyone had ever decided it was a good idea to install it in a public building. When this emergency was behind them, she'd tear it out herself.

"I was dealing with a call. Next thing I know, dude is standing over my desk, dripping bloody water all over the place. I called for the guys, and they took him to the back." Viviane threw a used paper towel into a red biohazard bag already filled with them. She nodded when Rebecca's jaw fell open. "Yeah, it was pretty bad."

"Is he why the ambulance is sitting out front?"

"No. They were already here, thank goodness. Bet their lights helped him find the station."

"As long as that big, boxy truck is out front, it'll act like a beacon and attract anyone who needs medical care of some kind but can't make it off the island." Greg popped the lid back onto the vacuum. He glanced pointedly at the coatrack along the wall with an oversized rubber mat laid out underneath it.

Taking the hint, Rebecca took off her raincoat and hung it up with the others, keeping the water contained to one place. "How serious are the injuries people come here with, and why here instead of the clinic?" She felt like she was in an alternate reality. Flooding she understood, but she hadn't made it to the section in the manual about what types of injuries people might sustain from flying debris or the storm surge.

Greg pushed the Shop-Vac into the corner and pulled a rubber mat in front of the doors. Dropping it, he kicked it into position. "Broken bones, sprains, possible concussions, things like that, mostly. But then you'll see random cuts, even a few puncture wounds. Health center's already diverting patients, so anyone with minor injuries knows not to go there."

"Your normal collection of injuries that happen when people try to rush in dangerous weather or don't consider their surroundings when taking shelter." A woman in a dark blue uniform walked up from the back, carrying a red biohazard bag. Her green eyes ran over Rebecca as she approached. "Also, there are the folks who insist on going outside to see what it's like to be in a hurricane. I've never understood that group. And finally, there're the injuries that come from construction, as people board up for the storm, and from car wrecks when people race to stay ahead of the worst of it."

Rebecca nodded. That all made sense. "Sheriff Rebecca West. Good to meet you."

"Sandra Baker. I wish it were under better circumstances. I've heard a lot about you."

"How's our..." she looked to Viviane, who shrugged, "*witness* doing? I assume you were checking him out."

Witness seemed the safest term, since they couldn't be sure if he was a victim. And without a victim, they couldn't call him a perp.

Baker used the back of her wrist to brush a stray strand of hair out of her eyes. It was a habit most medical professionals formed to keep their gloves from getting contaminated. "He's definitely in shock. Looks like he was in an accident, based on the injuries to his face. If I had to guess, and I've seen a lot of similar injuries, I'd say he got smacked pretty good by an airbag. Noticed what looked like airbag dust on his clothes too."

Sandra stuffed her red bio bag into the one Viviane was using, followed by her gloves. "We got him changed out of his wet clothes. He wasn't much help with that, so we had to do some cutting. Deputy Hudson bagged the clothes and is trying to get the witness to sip a little warm water now. One of your people kindly offered some hot chocolate, but any caffeine would only make his shock worse." She latched shut the medical bag that she'd set on Viviane's reception desk.

Rebecca grinned. "You mean hot chocolate doesn't fix everything?"

Sandra laughed. "I wish. We'd have IVs full of it, if it did."

"So...is our witness well enough to talk?"

Sandra waved her hand in a so-so gesture. "Not really. He's conscious but nonverbal, though I don't think he has a concussion or any serious injuries. It might take him a while. I've got him wrapped in a blanket. I don't think he's in immediate medical distress. The shock seems more emotional.

Aside from that and the wounds to his face, he's also got a sore spot on his back that might turn into a bruise later, but that's about it. We could take him to the hospital, but I doubt he'd be a priority right now. And frankly, I hate to take him over the bridge and leave the island with one less ambulance."

"What should we do if he gets worse?"

Sandra glanced out the window and frowned. "We'll sit outside until we get a call. If anything happens, radio us, and we'll come back in. In the meantime, keep offering the warm water and maybe a little bit to eat. The shock should begin to wear off and he'll probably start talking then."

"Were you able to estimate how much blood he had on him?" It was a long shot, but Rebecca was feeling hopeful.

"Do you mean if he had enough on him to be a lethal amount?" Sandra shook her head. "I wouldn't care to even guess, honestly. That's not really my area of expertise."

"I don't suppose you found any ID? Or might recognize him?" Rebecca's optimism refused to wane.

"You'd have to ask your deputy about that." The paramedic adjusted her chestnut brown hair, pulled tightly into a bun. "My preference would be to take him to the community health center, but they're already diverting, so I'm afraid we need to leave him here. I realize that's not ideal, but my partner and I will be out front until we're called away."

Rebecca sighed, resigned to accept the twists and turns of a natural disaster. She stopped Sandra as she donned her heavy raincoat. "I'm sorry to have to do this to you, but can you write up a witness statement about what you saw?"

"Yeah, no problem. I have to do this kind of thing all the time, so don't worry about it. If you don't mind, I'll do it in the truck. Gotta be on hand in case someone else calls in."

"That'll be fine."

"Oh, and if you get an ID on the man, can you relay it to me for my report?"

"Sure thing."

Baker nodded and pulled up her hood before heading back out.

Seconds later, Hoyt Frost's wife appeared at the gate separating the waiting area from the bullpen. A broad, welcoming smile lit up her freckled face. "Well, hello there."

"Hi. What brings you out in these conditions?"

Angie Frost held two steaming cups of what looked like coffee and craned her neck to look behind Rebecca. She was a pretty woman with youthful features, and it always amazed Rebecca that she had two grown sons and had been married to Hoyt for twenty-six years.

Knowing who she was likely looking for, Rebecca shook her head. "Hoyt's still out sandbagging."

"Well then, you'll just have to start without him."

Rebecca perked up as she took the cup Angie extended. Coffee was just what she needed. But the cup was unusually heavy, and when she glanced down, she found it filled with a thick, cream-colored liquid peppered with black flakes. Not what she was expecting.

"What's this?"

Angie handed her a spoon. "Biscuits and gravy. Eat up. You need nourishment. Bagging is taxing work. I know how you get wet all the way to the bone working those lines. Make sure you change your socks too."

Despite having two grown sons out on their own, apparently Angie Frost couldn't turn off her motherly tendencies.

Rebecca smiled at her concern. Using the spoon to poke into the gravy, she unearthed the biscuit occupying half the cup. Her stomach growled, and her fingers tingled as they warmed. Scooping up a portion of biscuit slathered in thick gravy, Rebecca took a bite.

She moaned, and her eyelids fluttered at the creamy concoction. "You're hired. Viviane, take note, we're swapping out Frosts."

"Yes, ma'am." Viviane giggled before returning her attention to the buzzing phone lines.

"Oh, hush you." Angie's cheeks turned a lovely shade of pink. "Being new, you might not know this, but the station becomes the meeting spot for everyone during bad weather. We like to make sure we have plenty to eat and drink. Things can get hectic."

"Mm...maybe hurricanes aren't so bad after all."

Angie motioned over her shoulder before depositing the second cup next to Viviane. "I have a whole slow cooker in the lounge, and there's coffee too."

Rebecca licked the back of her spoon. "This is fantastic. I'll be back for more after I've talked to our witness."

Greg nodded toward the back. "Hudson's with him."

Moving through the bullpen to the fresh pot of coffee, Rebecca poured a cup, taking in her coworkers as she blew on the surface. The grim faces were more relaxed now that the blood had been removed.

As she watched, Greg plopped down into his chair and began sending messages on his phone. Probably to his fishing friends, if she had to guess. Viviane's voice was muted by the rain pounding on the roof of the building as she fielded numerous calls. And Angie had settled into her husband's chair with her own steaming cup of coffee.

"Hey, Sheriff?"

Rebecca focused her attention back on the dispatcher. "Yeah?"

"We're already getting reports of storm damage starting on the southern tip."

Rebecca's mind raced as she moved back toward the lobby. She wasn't sure how destructive storm damage could be. Never in her life had she been close to a hurricane. How much of it would fall on her department's shoulders to clean up? The department's manual had only mentioned the need to clear streets to keep evacuation routes open. Suddenly, she didn't feel as confident as she had a moment ago. "How bad is it?"

Viviane ran a hand through her jet-black hair. "About what you'd expect at this point. Garbage cans that weren't stowed went flying. Lawn chairs that weren't secured smashed into some parked cars a few blocks over. Broken windows too. But the worst of it is from some asshole who didn't secure his rigging, so there's a boat that hit the beach and flipped a few times. It got caught up in some trees before making it too far, though."

Angie muttered something about "dang fools."

Cursing behind her, Greg picked up his desk phone. "I'll have Jimmy pop over and get pictures of the wrecked boat and the name so we can write up the citation. We'll see about securing it too." He gave Rebecca a pointed look. "Boats can become projectiles in high winds. An idiot who doesn't moor one properly is just as likely not to secure the sail either."

The idea of a boat sail being caught by the same wind that had battered the cruiser the whole trip over was terrifying. "Hopefully, he's the only idiot who didn't do things correctly."

Greg nodded. "We'll get it nailed down. Don't you worry." He began to dial.

Since there was nothing she could do about flying boats right then, Rebecca was heading back to visit their mysterious guest when another call came in. She paused to listen, comforted by Viviane's voice as she prompted information from the caller.

"A downed tree across Anchor Drive," Viviane said, glancing up at Rebecca.

Anchor Drive was the street the station was on.

"Is there anyone in the car?" Viviane shook her head. "Do you see the driver around the vehicle?" Another headshake. "Can you describe the vehicle for me please?" She jotted the details down. "Thank you. I've got help on the way. Please go inside out of this weather and keep an ear on the news."

After she'd dispatched emergency services, Viviane blew out a long breath and handed over the description of the vehicle—a red Maserati. "Five bucks I know who the driver of the car is."

Rebecca had been thinking the same thing. "Our bloody gentleman visitor. Could explain the shock, but not the blood. The paramedic said he didn't have any extensive wounds."

Curiouser and curiouser.

Continuing to eat, she headed for the interrogation room, finishing the last bite of biscuits and gravy as she reached the door, balancing two cups in one hand. Ducking into the lounge area across from it, she set her cup on the table before moving to the closed door.

The little viewing window was closed, so she paused to listen.

No sounds came from the other side. Rebecca knocked softly with a knuckle. She wanted to be respectful. Whether he was a witness or a victim, she didn't want to further traumatize or embarrass him by walking in with his ass on full display, in case he hadn't finished changing into whatever the department had lying around.

Darian opened the door while keeping his body turned toward where she guessed the individual was sitting. Instead of speaking, Darian squeezed his six-two frame through the opening and pulled the door closed behind him.

She stepped back, giving him room.

"How is he?"

"Whacked." Darian grimaced, his dark eyebrows pinched. "Haven't been able to talk to him. Had to get him out of those wet clothes. Medical don't think he has a head injury but think he's in emotional shock. He looked half dead when he walked in because of all the blood on him. I can't tell if he's a bad guy or a good guy, but he's snapped."

"Snapped how?"

He ran a hand over his cropped curls. "Never seen anything like it, not even when I was deployed."

Well, that can't be good. She knew Darian had seen some terrible things. Awful enough that he carried some lingering PTSD.

"Did he have any ID on him?"

Darian bobbed his head toward her office. "I put all his belongings on the floor next to your desk for now. He had a driver's license. His name is Malcolm Jenner, age forty-seven. He's from Virginia Beach."

"On the mainland? What could be important enough for him to brave this storm?"

"No clue. And he's not talking. Like I said, I bagged all his clothes and personal effects and put them in your office. His cell phone is in there, too, though it's got one of those liquid detection notifications on the screen. After seeing his clothes, honestly..." He trailed off, and his eyes unfocused for a moment. "In my opinion, he looked like he'd been holding someone who was bleeding heavily. From the pattern I could make out on his clothes, that's what I think."

"But he'd been out in the rain, right?"

That was something Rebecca hadn't been able to understand. With the way the rain was lashing down, how had the man still been covered in so much blood?

"Yeah, but he was wearing a long poncho when he arrived. If he pulled it on after getting the blood all over him, the blood wouldn't have all washed off."

Turning on her heel, Rebecca headed back to her office. Inside, she squatted next to an array of plastic bags, each one taped shut and labeled. Reading over the labels, she found each article of clothing had been separately bagged. Another bag held the contents of his pockets. With a groan, she stood and fetched a pair of gloves from the box she kept in her desk drawer. She also grabbed a few additional evidence bags.

Gloved up, Rebecca opened the bag and pulled out his wallet. Right in front was his driver's license. She knew her deputy would have searched the rest of the wallet, but Rebecca repeated the steps anyway. An old, water-logged receipt that was faded and couldn't be read, two credit cards, a few dollars, and an insurance card. Not much help, but better than nothing.

Rebecca glanced over her shoulder. Darian was leaning against her doorframe, eating out of a paper cup. He jerked his head toward the interrogation room. "I asked Greg to watch our guy while I grabbed a quick bite."

She couldn't blame him. It was hard to resist the tempting aroma wafting from Angie's giant Crockpot. "Ya know, I never realized a hurricane meant getting my skin sand-blasted in the pouring rain on an empty stomach and eating out of paper cups at work."

Darian snorted but kept shoveling the biscuits and gravy into his mouth. "Everything tastes better during a storm."

Rebecca rose to her feet and held out the license to her deputy. "I don't suppose you know Jenner? I realize he's not a local, but have you seen him before?"

Hudson leaned over to look at the picture, despite having already met the man in the flesh. Shock and trauma could alter a person's features, after all.

At first glance, Rebecca hadn't recognized poor Robert Leigh after he'd lost his only child and then gone crazy enough to go on a killing spree.

Darian shook his head. "That's the same guy, but I don't recognize him."

With a nod, Rebecca returned the items to the evidence bag and resealed it. "We've got his name, at least. Maybe that will help snap him out of this. Unfortunately, we need to get these items to the lab as soon as we can. I'll send a copy to the paramedics too."

Darian stopped eating with the spoon still in his mouth. "How are we supposed to do that?"

"I have no idea." Rebecca pulled out Jenner's cell phone. The liquid notification was still on the screen. She put it on top of an evidence bag to dry out. "Why don't you give them a call and see what they suggest? The techs know more about this than I do. Ask for Justin Drake. He worked with us recently and knows his stuff."

"Look at the new kid, making connections!" Darian teased with a glint in his eyes.

The lights flickered as the wind rose to a shrieking pitch. "Let's move on this. If we need to send someone to the mainland, we need to do it fast."

"Yeah, there's no telling if the bridge will get damaged by the high winds or airborne debris." The spark in his eyes from only a moment ago faded. "I'll tell Locke we need him to make a run."

"Only if they need it immediately. We can't afford to lose anyone to high water or a giant wave. You go take care of that, and I'll see what I can learn from Mr. Jenner."

Darian shot her a little salute and headed back to his desk.

As the wind continued to shriek, Rebecca prayed the island wouldn't be cut off from the mainland.

4

Malcolm Jenner sat at the table in one of the hard metal chairs. Someone had managed to get him dressed in ill-fitting clothes from the lost-and-found bin. The swollen nose and blackened eye on the right side of his face contrasted starkly with his ashen skin. Paired with his trembling body, the signs were clear that he was in distress.

But is that because he killed someone or witnessed something horrific?

The borrowed clothes hung loosely on his frame. Rebecca was sure they would have fallen off if he hadn't been sitting. A blanket hung over his shoulders, and his hands clutched the frayed ends. Gray, threadbare slippers covered a pair of white athletic socks.

His arm muscles vibrated as he hugged himself, swaying rhythmically. The paramedic's assessment of shock was virtually unnecessary. Jenner was curled in on himself so fiercely that a pill bug would have been envious.

When Rebecca sat across from him, he didn't even flinch, unless you counted his spasming muscles. She glanced at

Greg, who was sitting at the end of the table, but he only shrugged.

"Sir?" She ducked her head, attempting to make eye contact.

No one was home. He stared through swollen eyes without seeing, almost without blinking.

She tried again. "Mr. Jenner, I'm the sheriff. Can you tell me what happened?"

No response. Let's start small.

"Malcolm, can you tell me why you're on Shadow Island?"

Blink. At least that was something.

"Do you know someone here?" Rebecca searched his face, but it revealed nothing. "You told my dispatcher that you thought you'd done something wrong. Can you tell me what you meant?"

Although Rebecca knew his dead eyes were a classic sign of shock, she began to wonder if she'd overlooked an impairment code on his driver's license indicating he was hard of hearing. Despite her years of experience—taking witness statements with the Bureau and seeing the devastation wrought on countless victims—she couldn't recall encountering anyone as unresponsive.

The EMT had told her the local health center was turning away all but the most urgent cases. Under normal circumstances, Rebecca would have sent this man to the hospital for observation before attempting to question him.

These circumstances were far from normal.

What to do?

One, she could send him to the health clinic anyway, but that created an extra burden on an already overtaxed system. Plus, the paramedic had medically cleared him.

Two, she could have him sent to the mainland, but again, that would mean the island would lose an ambulance and an officer, since she would need to send one of the deputies with them.

Shit. Shit. Shit.

With a soft sigh, Rebecca pushed her chair away from the table and rose to her feet. The clock might be ticking on a victim. She couldn't spare a single moment if someone's life was on the line. Nodding to Greg, she indicated he should follow her.

After leaving the interrogation room, she and Greg found Darian finishing a second helping of Angie's potluck.

"Has he been like that the whole time?"

Both men shook their heads. Eyeing his colleague's full mouth, Greg answered her question. "He was talking when he came in, but he didn't say much. Just that he thought someone was hurt. Or that maybe he'd hurt someone. He wasn't making sense about that part."

Darian offered more insight. "The ambulance crew started assessing him almost before I finished changing him out of his clothes. Between the blood and the state he was in, everyone was concerned the guy was seriously hurt. Assessing him became the priority. We wanted them to transport him, but Sandra said his injuries were minor, especially with the health center diverting patients anyway."

He leaned against the wall and crossed his arms. His late shift would normally be ending about now, but they'd all be on the clock for the foreseeable future. "The paramedics insisted we get him out of his wet clothes first. I didn't disagree. Still don't. Cold is a terrible combination with shock. It can kill you fast."

"Did he look injured when he showed up?"

Darian bobbed his head noncommittally. "Yeah? Kind of."

Greg shrugged his agreement.

"He was shaking so hard and there was so much blood, we all thought he was injured," Darian added. "My first thought was shock from blood loss. And the shiner hadn't really darkened yet, but his cheek and nose were starting to swell. He had some bruises, and his skin was cool to the touch. Still is, somewhat. But he did drink some of the hot water we gave him."

Rebecca thought that over.

"If it's not all gone, can you get him some of Angie's biscuits and gravy? That seemed to work all kinds of miracles for me. And let's get him some more hot water too. Baker said no caffeine, so just water until he improves."

Darian nodded. "Yes, sir."

She looked between her two deputies, her smile vanishing. "Gentlemen, no one goes in that room alone anymore. No one."

Darian bristled, standing up straight. "What about—"

"Not me either." Rebecca shook her head. "If he's in an altered mental state, there's no telling what could happen. We also need to consider the possibility that, if he doesn't come out of his shock soon, his physical health could take a nosedive. I don't want anyone put in the position where they're attacked or have to deal with a medical emergency on their own. With this storm raging so loudly, can you say for certain anyone would hear if you called out for help back here? And you might not be able to access your radios."

Darian's shoulders drooped, and his light brown eyes filled with concern. "Roger that."

"Sandra said she doesn't think he has a concussion, but I think we should watch for slurred speech, assuming we can even get him talking again. Vomiting or seizures or convulsions. Anything changes with him physically, let me know."

The furrow between Darian's eyebrows deepened. "Shit. I sure as hell hope we don't end up dealing with any of that."

Rebecca nodded. "Sandra felt fairly confident his shock was worse than any chance of a concussion. According to her, we just need to keep an eye on him. So long as the ambulance is out front and we've got medical staff on hand, I'm fine keeping him here for now."

But Jenner's mental state continued to concern her.

"Deputy Hudson, how good are you at submission holds?"

A tick that could have been the start of a smile pulled at Greg's lips.

"I only leave bruises if I want to. I can show you some if you want, but after I get Jenner some rations."

Rebecca chuckled to herself as the deputies headed toward the food. She didn't know a lot about her staff yet, but she believed there was a lot more to Darian Hudson than he was letting on. He had a sense of pride but, so far, hadn't shown a single hint of arrogance or bravado.

She'd met more than a few people like that over the years and each of them she'd taken pride in calling friends.

Rebecca brushed some dried sand from her cheek and let out a long breath. Her fondness for this tiny law enforcement staff was undeniable, but there'd be time for those thoughts later. Right now, a hurricane was bearing down, and she needed to learn as much as she could about Malcolm Jenner —and who or what had lost so much blood.

Before any evidence was blown away.

5

Malcolm Jenner was no angel, but he wasn't a bad guy either. He had a handful of parking and speeding tickets. There was even one for driving while texting, thanks to Virginia's recent law change. And back when he was a young man, he'd been arrested for pot possession—for smoking a joint while walking when a cop spotted him. No big deal.

According to his records and everything Rebecca had pulled up so far, he was no hardened criminal. He was just a man who occasionally did stupid things. But when it truly mattered, he'd acted like a competent, thoughtful adult.

Malcolm had shown up for every court appearance and paid every ticket. After getting too many speeding tickets, the man had even gone to classes to get points taken off his record. He knew how to cross his t's and dot his i's when it mattered.

He worked for a large pharmaceutical company, and he'd had the same address for the last twelve years. His Maserati luxury car was only a few years old and a little flashy for her tastes. The tickets said it was red, and she was betting it was candy-apple. Everything made it seem like he was a mostly stable man.

Rebecca was assembling the folder with all his pertinents when Darian came back. Checking Jenner's phone, she dropped it into its evidence bag and took it with her too.

"Locke's ready to make the run if we need him," Darian told her. "I told him to get all the vehicles weighed down, just in case."

Weighed down? She thought that was only for snow. She had so much to learn.

"Makes sense. We had to do the same thing in West Virginia, where I grew up."

"S'*no*w problem. I'd take a blizzard over this any day."

Rebecca laughed as she walked around her desk and motioned for him to follow her back to the interrogation room. Her phone buzzed. Without looking at the screen, she rejected the call and walked in to talk to a nonverbal man who couldn't even make eye contact.

On the table in front of Malcolm sat two cups. One had water and the other had a generous portion of gravy and bits of a broken-up biscuit. Neither looked to have been touched, as far as she could tell. No spoon.

Rebecca raised an eyebrow at Darian.

He stepped behind Malcolm, who was rocking in his chair, moving to the other side of the room, and drew his thumbnail across his throat.

Suicide prevention. That was sound reasoning. She gave him a nod as she sat in the other chair. Darian clicked the start button on the video recorder, and Rebecca stated the time, date, and occupants of the room before starting her questioning.

"Sir, we looked through your belongings." She started slow and gentle. "Can you confirm your name and address?"

Malcolm's rocking continued.

"Your name is Malcolm Jenner."

He had zero reaction to his name.

"You live in Virginia Beach. Does that sound familiar to you?"

His head twisted slightly to the side. She was getting somewhere.

"Can you tell me why you came to Shadow Island, Mr. Jenner?" She waited for a response of any kind.

His head twisted again, reminding her of a dog cocking its head to better understand its master. Maybe just hearing her voice was helping.

"Mr. Jenner, is this your phone?" Rebecca slid the bagged device across the table and into his line of sight.

"Mermaid."

Shocked, Rebecca looked at Darian. Jenner's voice had been so quiet that she wasn't sure she'd heard him correctly.

"What was that? Did you say *mermaid*?"

"Yes...mermaid." Malcolm's rocking increased, and his hands clutched together. His eyes stretched wide, and his mouth fell open in a silent scream.

Rebecca stood and nodded toward the door. Darian followed her out into the hall after stopping the video recorder. They left the door cracked to keep an eye on Jenner.

"Is he talking about the statue outside?" she whispered. "The mermaid isn't quite as large as the painted horse, but it's an attention-getter."

"I've no idea. There're tons of statues like that all over the region. He could be talking about any of them."

That didn't help narrow things down. She only knew of two such statues on the island, but then, she'd never paid much attention. "Did you find any traces in his clothes or person that indicated he was in the water or on the beach?"

Darian frowned but shook his head. "Nothing. But then

again, with the sand whipping through the air and rain saturating everything, I doubt we'd be able to tell the difference."

Rebecca knew he was right. She was still coated in a mix of dried, sandy saltwater. "Yet somehow, he managed to arrive covered in blood."

"Well, even with a poncho, I don't think he could have gone far in this mess," he gestured to the rear door of the station where sheets of rain raged, "and still been so bloody. If he had sand on him, it may have been cleaned off when the paramedics gave him the once-over."

"You raise an interesting point. Has anyone confirmed that the car that hit the tree is his?"

"Sorry, no. I've been babysitting him since the paramedics arrived. We've got a lot going on. Greg's currently trying to coordinate some fishing friends to check on the boats to make sure they're properly moored."

"Let's add double-checking the owner of the red Maserati to the list of things we need to do. Meanwhile, do you think we're wasting time trying to get him to talk? Someone out there needs help." Rebecca chewed her lip and stared at the bagged phone in her hands, glad to see the liquid detection notification was gone.

Making a hasty decision she hoped didn't bite her in the ass later, she turned and walked back in. She switched on the video recorder before moving next to the man.

"Mr. Jenner, this phone was found in your possession. Is it yours?" He didn't respond. "Did you use your phone to talk to your little mermaid?"

Malcolm's face turned in her direction, but he didn't answer, and he didn't meet her gaze.

"Malcolm, if I use your phone, can I find the mermaid?"

He nodded. Then he frowned as if he were confused. Tears welled in his eyes.

Rebecca pressed the button to unlock the phone through

the clear plastic bag. "Malcolm, can I use your face to unlock the phone?" This wasn't a black-and-white issue. Getting biometrics from a corpse was one thing. Getting it from someone who could be considered impaired was another.

But this man could, in fact, be a victim who had escaped something terrible. They didn't even have a crime they could point to yet. Hell, they didn't even know if the blood on his clothes was from a human.

Almost imperceptibly, Malcolm nodded.

"I need you to answer out loud, Mr. Jenner. Can I use your facial scan to unlock your phone? I need to go through it, so I can find your mermaid."

"Yes. Please. She's..." His voice trailed off on a sob.

Holding the phone up quickly, she captured his face before he buried it in his hands. The phone unlocked.

Rebecca stepped out of the room and swiped through the settings to disable the lock. Then she moved on to the apps, going straight to the maps. He'd reacted when she'd asked why he came to the island, so it seemed like a good guess.

And it was. The last address he'd entered had been a local one. Rebecca went to the closest computer and punched in the address.

"You got someone?" Darian asked over her shoulder.

"168 Sunrise Terrace."

Darian whistled. "That's a rich area. Not as rich as Sandcastle Court, but rich enough."

"That could be where our victim is. Or crime scene. Or whatever caused our guy to be covered in so much blood, it broke his mind."

Rebecca jotted down information. "I need to get there fast, in case someone's injured but still alive. This says Clare and Brady Munroe live there. Do you know them?" It only took another moment to pull up photos from their licenses.

"Nope. Want me to go start the cruiser?"

She shook her head. "You stay here. Tell Hoyt to meet me there. I want someone here who can handle Malcolm if he goes ballistic. I'm guessing you still remember your combatives training, right?"

It was a wild guess, but it proved true when he jerked his chin up. Combatives was the name for hand-to-hand training the Army provided to their soldiers. There was even the telltale sign of his shoulders straightening. A distinctive military bearing had been ingrained in him.

"Hooah." His response was forceful, but he followed it up with a tap to his forehead in a sloppy salute.

Darian was an Army man through and through.

"Have Greg make sure everyone has fresh batteries in their radios. Make sure a few of the volunteer leaders each have a radio as well. I'm going to take some with me in case I come across anyone else who needs one."

Her deputy gave a curt nod, leaving no doubt the task would be completed. She ducked into her office and grabbed a radio for herself and a holster to protect it from the elements.

Rebecca eyed the device before securing it, hoping she wouldn't need to use the vital lifeline.

6

"Shit."

Hoyt cursed as a sandbag slipped from its spot on the wall. Bending over, he picked it up again and set it in place on the pile. With a groan, he straightened, knuckling his sore back.

One of the muscles in his lower abdomen cramped, and he had to take a deep breath. He never should have gotten on the shovel line. He'd forgotten how many core muscles were used for the task.

Pushing his stomach out, he twisted with his elbows at shoulder height, trying to work out the fatigue that was building. His raw hands were a close second in the pain category.

"You doing okay there, Hoyt?"

Concern was written in Ryker Sawyer's tawny eyes as he jumped down from the truck that had brought the latest load of sand and was already mostly empty. The one good thing about working around the sand truck was the abundance of traction with no risk of slipping.

"I'm just old." He laughed as the younger man joined him.

Ryker's damp, sandy hair blew in the wind. "You need to take a break. You just had major surgery a couple weeks ago."

It wasn't a question, but Hoyt shook his head anyway.

"We need to get these levees built. Cars are already leaving. We can't have the roads flooding before everyone can get off the island."

"Yeah, well, you're not going to be of any help if you pull that appendectomy scar open. Are you even cleared to do this heavy lifting?"

"It wasn't supposed to be this heavy!" Hoyt razzed back. "But yeah, I've been cleared. Of course, I don't think the doc knew I'd be doing something like this right after getting my stitches out."

Yesterday, when he learned the hurricane was heading their way, he'd gone to the health clinic and gotten his stitches removed a day early. No sense in dealing with the itchy bastards while soaked to the skin.

He didn't know if this kind of exertion might cause issues. All the doctor had said was that he was cleared for full duty but to listen to his body. But if he listened to his body, he'd be kicked back on his porch, drinking beers and eating meals with Angie. Or maybe just lounging in bed. A comfy, dry bed was an especially appealing idea right now.

"If someone had filled these bags with dry sand, they wouldn't be so damn heavy! Then I wouldn't have to worry about popping a stitch. Maybe I should get back up in the truck and show you how to do it right, young man."

"Not sure if you've noticed it yet, old man, but," Ryker held his hands out palms up, "it's raining. Not much I can do about wet sand." He flipped his palms over, flinging the gathered water in his friend's face.

Hoyt laughed and had to press his hand against his scar as it started to twinge and pull. "I sure as shit hope I didn't overdo it." He leaned back against the side of the truck. "Don't tell Ange."

"If she asks, I ain't lyin'!" Ryker laughed and moved to take Hoyt's place in the line. "You've done enough, man. Plenty of others have joined us since you got here. Go have a seat, get a cup of coffee. Stop showing us younger ones up. Come back when you're rested. We're going to have to go get some more sand here in a bit anyway."

That sounded like a great plan. He could take a quick break in his GMC and maybe even put his feet up. A vibration at his waist made him groan. "Duty calls." He patted his side where his phone hung from a clip on his belt.

Ryker nodded. "Tell Rebecca I said hi."

Hoyt paused, hearing the wistful tone in his voice. A slow, knowing grin stretched his tired face. "I'll do that. Anything else you want me to tell her? Maybe write a note, and I can pass it to her after class?"

Ryker chuckled and ducked his head before walking off.

Hoyt couldn't see it, but he'd bet the young man was blushing. This was too good. A chance to rib both Ryker and West at the same time.

Whatever the call was about, he hoped it would give him an excuse to head back to the station. And not just so he could tell West what Ryker had said.

Angie had been cooking up a giant batch of her biscuits late last night, and he knew she'd have brought something to the station by now. His stomach rumbled in anticipation as he weaved through the assembled vehicles to his truck. Thankfully, no one had blocked him in.

With a sigh that ended in a groan, he fell into the driver's seat and struggled against the increasing gusts of wind to close the door. He reached for the police radio he'd installed in his old truck. Phones were persnickety during heavy rains, but his old reliable radio was always there for him.

"Did someone call me, Viviane?"

"Hold on, I think it was Darian." The woman had been fielding calls all night but had answered his call immediately. He wasn't sure if it was a good or bad sign that she could respond so quickly.

Darian took a few minutes to respond, and Hoyt used that time to further stretch out his back, forearms, and neck.

"Hoyt, Sheriff needs you to meet her out at 168 Sunrise Terrace. Possible location of a victim who sustained massive blood loss. Over."

"Sunrise? But that's not even on the tip. Did someone get in a wreck already? Over."

"No, it's related to a blood-covered man who walked in here a bit ago, muttering about needing help and finding a mermaid. Over."

"A what and a what?" Hoyt's face scrunched in confusion, and he felt the chafing windburn that was already settling in on his cheeks, along with the drying saltwater infused with wind-blown sand. "Are you shitting me?"

"No, sir. This storm churned up the crazies. Get out there and be her backup. Over."

"Roger that."

"And Frost?"

"Yeah?"

"Don't slip in the blood. Over and out."

Hoyt pulled up in front of the address, parking right behind the sheriff's cruiser. West had managed to beat him to the location but was still waiting in her Explorer to avoid the torrential rain. Her reflective coat was visible, even through the fast-moving windshield wipers. He took one final sip of his coffee to brace himself for getting wet all over again.

A quick prayer went up in the hope that Darian had been razzing him about the blood.

West stepped out at the same time Hoyt did and waited for him to join her.

"What we got here?" He had to lean in to make himself heard over the relentless wind.

West gestured toward the front door. With a nod, he followed her. It was clear from the lit porch light that the home still had power. Once under the protection of the covered porch, West rang the doorbell, briefing him as they waited for a reply.

"Not sure. We had a man walk in, covered head to toe in blood. He said he might have hurt someone. We got his name and traced him back here as his last known location. We suspect we know where his car is but aren't sure. With such low visibility, we may not find it until the hurricane passes."

"Are you talking about Brady Munroe? This is his house."

West shook her head. "No, the man who came into the station is Malcolm Jenner."

Hoyt sorted through his mental Rolodex of acquaintances. "Don't know him. What was Jenner doing here?"

"All we know about him so far is that this address was in his maps app on his cell phone. A crime may have been committed here."

"Hudson said there was a lot of blood. Tell me he was pulling my leg."

"Sorry to say, he wasn't. And besides being coated in blood, Jenner kept talking about a mermaid. Are there any mermaid statues nearby?"

"Not that I can think of. Not the big ones, at least. Plenty of people have them as garden decorations or wind chimes. This is a beach town. Mermaids are everywhere around here, including shop windows."

She rang the doorbell again before pounding her fist on

the door. "Well, I'd have preferred to roll up on this house and find a large mermaid statue to tie Malcolm Jenner more closely with this residence. But I guess we're not that lucky. We do have his phone indicating this address was of interest to him, so let's keep an eye open for anything suspicious. And for any mermaids."

He rubbed his jaw. "'Cause that will be easy in this weather. I wouldn't be able to spot a mermaid before she slapped me with her tail." Hoyt peered at the house numbers next to the door. "Are you sure this is the right address? The GPS could get it wrong. The Munroes both work long weeks off the island. Might not even be home. This could have been a burglary gone wrong."

"Well, it's the only clue we've got, so let's hope it pans out and we're in time to save whoever lost all that blood." The glint in her eye indicated she was about to spill the beans on something terrible. "The blood wasn't his. We don't know where it came from."

Squaring her shoulders, West rang the doorbell a third time. When no one answered, Hoyt balled up his fist and pounded hard enough to rattle the frame.

Even over the strengthening storm and intense wind, the Munroes should have heard that and responded.

If they could.

7

Rebecca pounded both fists against the door, then placed her ear against it, listening for anything in response. Not hearing a single sound, she called out again, "Sheriff's Department! Wellness check. Please answer the door."

All they got was the gale-force winds whipping at them with stinging rain and the heavy crash of the tide tearing at the beach somewhere out of sight.

"Maybe they already evacuated?" Hoyt moved to look through the windows.

"Maybe. You said they both work on the mainland, so maybe they just decided not to return until the storm passed. Maybe they're smarter than the rest of us."

"Or maybe they've had a close call with a rogue wave or were almost washed off the road by storm surge." Hoyt spoke as if from personal experience.

Rebecca shuddered. How was he so calm? If she didn't have to be on the island, she'd have left for the safety of somewhere inland. She could just ride out the storm while reading a good book in a café.

"Go around the side and see if you can find any sign of anything. Good or bad. Keep an eye out for indications they might have left too."

Hoyt nodded and took off for the side of the house. His dark outerwear disappeared into the gloom within a few steps, leaving her alone on the porch.

Turning back to the door, she leaned into it and continued to slam her fist on it, hoping to attract someone's attention. "Clare and Brady Munroe, this is the sheriff! Please answer the door if you are able or call out if you cannot get to the door."

Not that she would be able to hear them if they did call out, but she had to keep yelling and hope she was heard. What if they were inside calling out for help, and she simply couldn't hear them? Their voices might be muffled by the rain or a gag, or they were simply unconscious and bleeding out.

Rebecca pressed her ear to the wood and slowed her heart rate. She tried to block out the sounds of the storm and focus only on any sounds inside by closing her eyes. She pressed her hand against her other ear to that end.

There was nothing. Only slight vibrations from the wind.

Moving away from the door and off the porch, she pulled her hood back up and took out her flashlight. Pointing the light at an angle, she checked the windows along the front. No lights were visible inside the home on the first floor. The second floor was another story. Two windows cloaked in drapes indicated a light was on in at least one upstairs room.

She approached the living area window. Even with her face pressed against the glass and her hands cupped around her face, she couldn't see in well enough to identify anything other than basic shapes. That blob in the corner could be a plant, a bookcase, or a body leaning against the wall. Or it could be a shadow from any of the multitude of things stuck to the glass. She wiped the torn leaves and detritus from the window and peered again. No luck.

Using her palm, she slapped the glass, again calling out for anyone to answer. It seemed no one could hear her cries.

She jumped when someone grabbed her left shoulder, spinning to face them.

Hoyt leaned forward and yelled, "I was calling to you, but I guess you couldn't hear me. I saw blood on the back deck and a sign of a fight in the kitchen. We've got more than enough to go in now."

"Did you check the door?"

He gave her an *of course I did* look. "Yeah. Locked."

Rebecca ran back to the front door with Hoyt hot on her heels. With her left hand, she pulled her coat up and out of the way, freeing access to her gun holster. Standing to the side of the door with her Armory 1911 in hand, she gripped the doorknob. She nodded to Hoyt, and he mirrored her position on the other side of the door, his Glock drawn and his powerful flashlight switched on.

With one strong kick, the door swung open. She was often astonished at how flimsy locks could be.

Peering around the doorframe with Hoyt providing illumination, Rebecca crouched slightly as she pointed her gun. "Sheriff! Coming in! Call out if you can hear me." Even as she yelled, she took slow, careful steps into the house.

Like so many other high-end beach homes, the house had an open layout. She could see through the front sitting room and into the oversized kitchen and adjoining breakfast room from the doorway.

Hoyt stepped up beside her and nodded to his left.

She nodded back and stepped forward and to the right. Their lines of sight overlapped with each step they took forward and covered every angle of the rooms. Glancing down, she stepped carefully over drops of blood that stretched from the staircase to the kitchen. Drip trail. Someone had been dripping blood as they moved through the house.

While Rebecca knew she could be treading on evidence not visible to her, their priority was to clear the house and check if there was someone to save.

Communicating silently, Rebecca and Hoyt moved around each other, sweeping the rooms one by one. Several rooms showed signs of a disturbance, from bloody marks to knocked-over furniture. Even the dining room table had been knocked askew. Considering that it appeared to be solid oak and could seat at least eight people, it would have taken more than a simple bump to accomplish that.

While blood painted the walls in a few spots in the front room, in the back of the house there was a pool of dark liquid on the tile floor near the large cooking island. Cast-off splatter and drip stains.

Rebecca tried to make sense of the scene and what she knew of Jenner's injuries. Baker had speculated that the injuries to his face had been caused by a car's airbag. Until they found his car, or the man started talking, Rebecca couldn't know for sure.

The scene in front of her clearly indicated an altercation. But other than the injuries to Jenner's head and face, the only bruise the EMT had found on Malcolm was on his back. Could his injuries indicate he'd initiated a fight? Or had he fended off an attack? More questions without answers.

Off to the side of the breakfast room was a sliding glass door. Streaks along the wall indicated someone had brushed against the plaster on their way to this door. On the handle was more blood.

A few feet in from the door was a blob of something dark and slimy. Before she could do more than ascertain that no one was lurking on the porch, they moved on. Sand crunched under her feet as she turned the last corner. There was a bathroom and what looked to be a small guest room with an en suite.

Rebecca cleared both of those while Hoyt stayed in the hallway, watching her back and the final section of the house to be searched.

When she joined him again and nodded that she was ready to proceed, he raised his voice as they moved as a unit back to the stairs. "Sheriff's department. We're coming up. Call out if you can hear us."

Not waiting for a response, they took the stairs slowly and carefully, constantly checking above and below as the second floor came into view. Hoyt took the lead.

Avoiding the blood trail was trickier here. Though the stairs were wide enough for them to walk side by side, they were also dotted with numerous drops of blood. Rebecca silently groaned, knowing their coats were dripping water as they walked over the evidence. There was simply no way to preserve the crime scene under the circumstances.

"Sheriff's department! Call out if you can hear my voice. Does anyone need assistance?" Hoyt's head swiveled to the two doorways they could see from their position.

Rebecca squeezed up beside him, ready to cover his back whichever way he decided to go. When no one responded, he dipped his chin, indicating the smaller door that was slightly ajar. The other one was a closed double door, probably the master bedroom, with faint light emanating from within. Rebecca nodded, covering the larger door while crouching on the top stairs as he moved to clear the other room.

There was no way to keep an eye on both directions at the same time. Rebecca tried to hold Hoyt's location in the back of her mind, listening for any sounds he might make. But the storm was louder now that they were closer to the roof, and she couldn't hear anything other than the heavy rain pounding as it pelted the structure.

He called out from several feet behind her. "Clear."

Rebecca nodded, stepping up and taking the lead but staying crouched, so she wasn't in the way of his gun. Once she'd ascended, she again stepped right, and Hoyt moved up on her left. They moved silently to the last room of the house.

Together, they approached the closed double door. Using her foot, Rebecca shoved one door open. Light flooded into the hallway, assaulting her senses. It was followed by an overwhelming stench.

"Holy shit. It smells like a slaughterhouse."

Her whisper was only a breath before Hoyt cried out, "Fucking hell. That's Clare."

On the bed was a dead woman. She lay in a pile of twisted and rumpled, blood-soaked sheets with skin so red she appeared to have been painted with her own plasma. Numerous stab wounds punctured her torso. Her breasts were covered in large purple clamshells, and her face was brightly painted with cosmetics.

The handle of a knife protruded from her chest between the shells. Someone had twisted her legs to the side, wrapping them in barbed wire and driftwood to form a crude tail.

They'd found Jenner's mermaid.

8

Leaning over the bed, Rebecca took another close-up picture of the mermaid Clare Munroe had been crafted into. It was a gross combination of fairy tale and horror show.

This time, she focused on the victim's hair and all the things wrapped within the strands. While most of her hair was dry, sections were damp where seaweed, sand, and broken shells had been twisted and woven in.

There was also a smattering of the same beachy items liberally sprinkled over her body and the bed. Someone killed her, then dumped beach scraps all over her. The shells on her breasts hadn't come from the beach, however. They'd been painted purple and had holes drilled into them for strings that would have been tied around her neck and chest, like a clamshell bikini top. Rebecca surmised they'd been purchased.

The purple color matched Clare's glittery eye shadow that had been artistically applied along with the blue-green lipstick. Both of which had been smeared during the struggle. The single starfish earring in one ear and the splotch of blood on the other earlobe also indicated a fight.

It hadn't been visible from the door, but there was another pool of blood between the bed and the bathroom. A single line of cast-off blood on the ceiling indicated that Clare had been stabbed at least once while standing there before the knife was pulled out.

Rebecca had already photographed that before she'd gone into the bathroom. In there, she'd found a discarded fabric mermaid tail hanging up. It was so much nicer than the barbaric metal and scrap wood one that had been fashioned to her corpse.

Taking in her surroundings, Rebecca had a theory.

Clare had been dressing herself up in her mermaid costume for some reason. Then she'd been jumped and stabbed while leaving the bathroom and fallen onto the bed. While on the bed, she was stabbed repeatedly. There were slashes in the fabric and even puncture holes in the mattress around her.

Some were dry, indicating they were missed strikes. Others were filled with blood. Without flipping her over to check, there was no way to verify that. But that was a job for the M.E. once she arrived. *If* she arrived.

The cuts in the chest and abdomen were long and deep. Judging by their size and the handle, she was betting a common kitchen knife had been used.

"A weapon of opportunity then, not a planned attack." She leaned over and tried to get another shot of the handle. It was distinctive, and she could probably match it to a brand later.

"This whole place looks like a madhouse, so that's not surprising."

Hoyt had walked up behind her, having ditched his raincoat by the front door. She'd done the same after they'd secured the scene and retrieved their evidence kits from the cruiser. There was no sense in tracking even more water inside and further contaminating the evidence.

"Or something straight out of *Grimms' Fairy Tales*. Have you read the original little mermaid? It's brutal."

"Can't say that I have."

"It's dark." She shuddered at Hans Christian Andersen's version. "But her death was nothing as twisted as this."

"When I was snapping photos in the kitchen, I found a clump of seaweed by the sliding glass door. What the hell happened here?"

Rebecca glanced over at him and shrugged. The scene told some of the story, but not what led to it all.

"I'm glad you got the pictures. Forensics won't be able to make it out. They suggested we take as many photos as we can, bag the small stuff, and seal up each room and then the house. I'd like to do a video walkthrough, too, just to make sure we get everything. They'll come over once they can safely make it across the bridge."

"Not going to do a whole hell of a lot of good to tape the doors if the windows blow out. Or in. Or the roof gets ripped off." Hoyt moved beside her. He was holding a camera of his own. "I only took preliminary photos of the scene, since I was hoping forensics would somehow make it here. But I've got my tape measure and can go back and take new ones with references for scale."

"Thanks. That would help."

Hoyt rubbed his five o'clock shadow. "I came up to tell you the ambulance is here. I also called the station, and Jenner is as fine as a catatonic man can be."

"Maybe he'll come out of it soon. Bailey won't be happy when she hears how unusual this one is. Still, it's better than leaving Mrs. Munroe here."

"After what was done to her, she deserves as much respect

as we can give her." His voice was soft and filled with heartache.

Rebecca was reminded that her deputy knew the victim. He'd said as much, but she'd forgotten in the flurry of clearing the house and then rushing to gather evidence. A quiet sadness pulled at his eyes as he stared at the dead woman.

"Shit, Hoyt, I'm sorry. You said you knew her?"

"Not well. Just enough to say hi when I saw her at the grocery store or the movies." He shook his head. "As I said, she and her husband both travel a lot for work. Brady more so. She was a fan of those rom-coms Angie is always dragging me off to see and the two of them used to compare notes."

A voice called out from the hallway. "Are we clear to come up?"

Hoyt headed to the top of the stairs. "Yeah. Come on up."

Sandra Baker and her partner walked into the room, carrying a body bag and a medical kit. They ignored everything else and only had eyes for the victim.

"Well, shit."

Rebecca nodded at the startled paramedic, glancing at his name badge. Kendric Hayes. "That's what I said too."

"Is that...barbed wire?" Sandra carefully shuffled closer to Rebecca, who backed out of her way. "Where in the hell would it come from?"

Rebecca had no idea. "It's very rusty, so I'm guessing it was found on the beach with the other detritus, like the fishhook in her hair."

"I'm going to go get the protective sleeves. I don't want to risk getting stabbed on that barbed wire. Jesus, there's blood everywhere." Kendric shook his head with a frown and turned to leave.

"You can wrap her up in the sheet too. Take as much of the bed linens as you need to."

"You sure about that?"

"Yup. They're already pulled from the corners in two places. Forensics isn't coming today. Once we get the body to the hospital, we can remove the bedding in a clean environment, maybe find some evidence too. I don't want you guys getting stabbed through the bag when you carry her back down. There's blood on all of it. And if the bag is punctured, that poses a problem for all of us."

Sandra stepped around to the side of the body. She leaned over Clare Munroe, looking for the best way to approach a potentially dangerous situation. "Where are we taking her?"

"The hospital or health center or whatever they call it here."

"So long as they have a place to store her and someone who will sign for the body, that's good enough for us." Sandra unzipped the body bag.

Rebecca's phone rang, and she pulled it out to check the caller ID. It was the same number that had been calling her all morning. Maybe if she answered, they'd stop calling.

"Sorry guys, I've got to take this." Rebecca motioned with her phone and got waved off by both paramedics.

"We'll take care of this. You go do what you need to do."

Rebecca stepped out into the hallway and made for the other room. "Sheriff West here. How can I help you?"

"You could start by answering your phone when I call you." She didn't recognize the voice, but Rebecca recognized the tone as coming from a man who thought he owned the island.

She took a guess. "Is this Mr. Vale?"

He snorted, and she knew she was right.

"Of course it is."

Of course? Has he forgotten they hadn't yet met because he'd been on vacation the past several weeks?

"WHAT CAN I do for you, sir?"

"As previously mentioned, you can start by answering your damn phone when I call. "I've been calling you over and over."

"I've been a little busy, sir. First, I was working the sandbag line, and then I was dealing with a mysterious man covered in blood who couldn't even tell me his name. And now, I'm trying to process the scene of a brutal murder possibly connected to that man. And it isn't even six."

Richmond Vale grunted but didn't respond for a moment. It was a lot to take in, after all.

"That does sound like a bad morning, but we're all having a bad morning. The entire island is. We need you to come down here so we can coordinate the evacuation process. Boris isn't slowing down any. In fact, he's gaining speed. We need to make a decision, and we need to do it as quickly as possible. But we can't do that until you show up."

Rebecca cursed under her breath. Had Vale been calling for a different reason? After all, the Select Board was supposed to be voting on whether to keep her as the sheriff in a few hours. The town's quirky charter allowed the Select Board to appoint a full-fledged sheriff between election cycles. With all hell breaking loose, that vote wasn't going to happen today.

"Mr. Vale, is there any way this can be done over the phone? I'm at a crime scene and can't be pulled away."

He snorted, and she could picture him waving his hand in the air dismissively. "Ms. West, the people of this island need you. I think a corpse can wait. If you want to be named sheriff, you need to start acting like one."

Rebecca ignored the jab. She was doing her job. Sheriffs investigated crimes. Planning for natural disasters was not something she'd learned at Quantico.

Sometimes, she wondered why she'd even wanted the role. "Sir, are you at town hall?" Rebecca stared out the window, ignoring the beautiful happy couple in the pictures that seemed to take up every inch of space in this office.

"Of course. You need to get here as soon as possible. It's already six. Reports still have Boris making landfall around four this afternoon, but he's gaining in intensity. I predict a mandatory evacuation coming soon, and I want to get ahead of it."

Rubbing her forehead between her eyebrows, she tried not to let him hear her sigh. "Sir, I'll leave as soon as I can. I need to coordinate things here first."

"We have more than a thousand *living* people who need to be evacuated to a safe location. Their safety trumps your case, I'm afraid. I must insist you come now."

As much as she hated agreeing with Vale, he was right. She had to leave the crime scene to Hoyt and the paramedics. "I'll be there as soon as I drop evidence back at the station."

"Now, Sheriff West."

"Sir, with all due respect, I simply cannot do that. I am required to secure this evidence. Leaving it sitting in my cruiser in a parking lot during a hurricane is not secure."

He didn't bother to hide his exasperated sigh. "Then get here as soon as you can after you do that."

"Are you certain we can't do this over the phone, under the circumstances?"

"Sadly, no. We double-checked. All votes asking the governor for disaster assistance must be taken in person."

Which was why they'd been trying to get in touch with her since word of their island being in the path of Boris had made the news. "Fine. I'll get there as soon as possible."

Rebecca hung up and went back to the master bedroom. Not finding Hoyt and not wanting to watch the paramedics deal with the corpse, she went searching.

She caught up with him in the kitchen. He was taking pictures of every inch and marking notes for direction and measurements. It was going to be one hell of a task, cataloging every blood drop and smear on his own, but she didn't have a choice.

"You done talking with your boyfriend?" He shot her a teasing grin.

"Oh, don't let the chairman of the Select Board hear you call him that."

Hoyt was undeterred at the name drop. "What did that charmer want?"

"How on earth did that guy get elected as chairman when no one seems to like him?"

Her deputy shrugged. "Don't know. So what bee is up his butt in the middle of all this?"

"Apparently, my presence is required over at town hall for an in-person vote. We're formally asking the governor for disaster assistance. And I'm betting he'll ask to approve mandatory evacuation early, so he can tell the media his residents got to safety earlier than planned, thanks to his insistence."

"Shit. I knew it was bad. How much worse has it gotten?"

"I'll get an update while I'm over there. Right now, I need to get the evidence I have back to the office and then bolt to town hall. I plan to discuss evacuation plans with everyone there."

An uneasy feeling settled in as Rebecca surveyed this portion of the crime scene. If Clare had been killed in her bedroom, who got into the physical fight in the kitchen? Had the fight started there, then Clare ran upstairs to what she thought was the safety of her bedroom? Only to be hacked to death?

Her line of thinking was cut short as Hoyt gave a relieved sigh. She felt even more guilt. How many people had been waiting to hear about evacuation orders before deciding to leave their homes?

Has avoiding Richmond Vale's calls put people's lives in danger?

Hoyt snapped her out of her spiraling thoughts. "You mind if I make a suggestion?"

Rebecca could have hugged him but nodded instead. "Please."

"My recommendation is to go with plan A. It's straightforward, misses all the current problem spots, and takes residents through the areas we've already bolstered."

Her instincts had been right. It was the plan she thought would work best too.

"Plan A. I saw that when I was reading over the map. Excellent suggestion. Thanks." A copy of the map was in her cruiser. She could reference that when talking to the board. It never hurt to come prepared.

"No prob, Boss. And remember, don't show fear." He flared his nostrils comically. "They can smell it."

Rebecca laughed and picked up her box of evidence to haul to the cruiser. First a bloody zombie, then a gruesome, macabre crime scene, and now a conversation that could impact the lives of everyone on the island.

Time to sink or swim.

9

Rebecca stared at the parking lot lights, which would normally have switched off automatically with the dawn. But the sunrise an hour ago went unnoticed. The clouds seemed to have dropped from the sky. Sheets of rain carried by the now-steady wind had only gotten stronger since she'd left her home about four hours earlier. Visibility was nonexistent.

Here goes nothing.

Pulling her hood up, she cinched it tight. There was no waiting for a break in the downpour this time. Rebecca shoved a few two-way radios into her coat pockets and tightly gripped the plastic-coated evacuation map before flinging open the Explorer's door.

She groaned as the wind tried to slam it back, and it took more of her power than she would have liked to wrestle her way out of the vehicle. Once she had her feet on the ground, the wind changed, and she struggled to close the damn thing.

A sharp crack on the top of her head nearly knocked her to her knees, and she lifted her arms to shield her face and head as she ran for the town hall. Small branches and other objects she couldn't identify ripped through the air.

Inside, the floor was wet, and she had to grab the doorframe to keep from slipping as she rushed through.

As her shoes squeaked on the floor, heads popped up like flowers after a rain. Dozens of people milled around folding tables set up around the room, seemingly at random. One table held trays of sandwiches and urns of coffee. The others had stacks of papers, clipboards, and boxes of pens.

Rebecca saw what she needed and headed for the coffee urns while shedding her outerwear.

A shorter man with dark, slicked-back hair hurried over to intercept her. He almost looked as if he matched everyone else who had been working outside today until she realized his hair was covered in gel and not rainwater. His pants weren't even wet at the cuffs. She recognized him from his picture right away.

Richmond Vale's connections to the Yacht Club were enough for her to loathe him for a few lifetimes. But add in his lack of concern for others and his overwhelming desire to control people, and she could barely stand to be around the man.

She didn't want his stink on her.

"Sheriff West, good of you to finally join us." His lips were pursed, and he had a nest of wrinkles on his forehead. "It appears you have little regard for the safety of the good people of Shadow Island."

Rebecca slowed at his approach. The crowd in the room stared at them, anticipating a confrontation.

Nice to meet you too...not.

"That's an interesting way of looking at things."

She managed to keep her words civil. This was, after all, one of the people who would eventually have a vote on her status as sheriff. Despite all her grumping this morning, she honestly wanted to keep this job. The people of this island had quickly become her family, and she cared about them more than she realized once Boris became a threat. Rebecca knew she'd do anything to protect them.

"When the roads on our main evacuation route started flooding, while cars were trying to make it through, I thought it was essential I tackle that problem first."

"Sheriff, while I appreciate your work ethic and willingness to get down in the trenches with everyone else, I have to disagree." Mayor Ken Doughtie appeared by her side, beer gut sticking out like he'd swallowed a keg. He gave her a nod but didn't smile.

She nodded in return. "How so?"

"Nearly anyone else on this island could have filled or stacked those bags. But only we," Mayor Doughtie gestured around to the men and woman, "can formally ask the governor of the great Commonwealth of Virginia to provide disaster assistance. I understand you thought you were doing what was best, but if you're going to be the sheriff, you need to look at the island as a whole. That includes the administrative side of things."

Despite his words, the mayor had sand stuck in the cuff of his trousers.

He caught her gaze and looked down. "I answered my phone when I was called." He gave her a pointed look.

Suitably chastened, Rebecca nodded. "I did answer my pager as soon as it rang. Calls on my personal phone, I ignored."

The mayor frowned and turned to Vale. "Where's the sheriff's work phone? Have we been using her private number this whole time?"

The chairman shrugged. "Wallace's was deactivated, per protocol. I'm sure a replacement has been ordered."

"Until that happens, let's keep our work calls to her pager, then. Did we even bother calling the station and asking dispatch where she was?"

Watching Vale's face screw up in annoyance at the mayor's questions almost made this trip worthwhile.

"That's a problem for a different time." Vale waved them off. "Right now, we need to vote on asking for the governor's assistance."

This is ridiculous. Why vote on something so damn obvious? Maybe it makes their little dicks feel bigger.

"I vote we make the request." The mayor gave a definitive answer.

"I also vote for assistance. By now, the flooding should have been diminished by the levees we built. But there are already widespread reports of damage. The bridge is passable but may not be for long." Rebecca was happy she had something to add to the conversation. "Authorities in Coastal Ridge are already blocking off traffic on their end of the bridge, so we can use all lanes to leave."

"Perfect!" Margaret Darby appeared from a hallway and gave Rebecca a warm smile, her resemblance to Viviane obvious.

Viviane's mother seemed to be a matriarch of the community and often popped up exactly when she was needed.

Rebecca was calmed by her appearance. "Mrs. Darby, I wasn't expecting to see you here."

"I go where I'm needed, dear." She handed a clipboard to the mayor. "And please, call me Meg."

"That's two votes asking for aid from the commonwealth. Mr. Vale, would you like to add your vote to make it official and unanimous?"

"Yes, of course."

Vale opened his mouth to continue, but Meg cut him off.

"Perfect. I expect Mayor Doughtie will make that call immediately. Right, Ken?"

"Sure thing."

Meg continued to take command of the assembled group. "I took the search grid Darian Hudson set up and modified it for our needs. We'll only need twelve people and three cars to get this done." She pointed at the clipboard she'd just handed over, tracing her finger over a path Rebecca couldn't see. "Once the siren is sounded," she pointed to Rebecca, "then we can start knocking and getting people out of their homes. We'll wait an hour and send the second group to look for stragglers."

"But what evacuation route will we tell everyone to use?" Vale's tone dripped with superiority.

"Is there a road other than the bridge I don't know about?" Rebecca asked, wading into the conversation. "I think we should go with plan A. It's straightforward, misses all the current problem spots, and we've spent the morning bolstering it."

Meg and the mayor gestured that they agreed, and even Vale gave a tiny nod. Rebecca would have to remember to thank Hoyt for confirming this was the best route.

"City works will switch over all the traffic lights to flashing." Rebecca reached for the clipboard, and the mayor handed it over. "Barrels and cones won't work. We'll need cruisers with lights on and everyone wearing reflective vests. If any spare firetrucks are available, they can help block off roads we don't want people traveling on."

Rebecca glanced at the map in her hands and then longingly at the coffee urns.

"Hun, have you not gotten something warm to drink?" Meg glared at Vale. "She has time for that, for lord's sake, Dick!"

"It's Rich. Not Dick." Spittle flew from his mouth as his cheeks flushed.

"Then stop acting like one!" Meg snapped back just as fast and twice as loud.

Rebecca couldn't stop her smile, so she turned and headed for the coffee instead.

Meg huffed and followed her, and so did the mayor.

"Sorry about that, Rebecca. I should have realized you've been too busy to grab anything." Doughtie tugged his pants up under his beer gut. "How bad is it out there?"

"I've never seen anything like this…and I'm gathering it's going to get worse before it gets better." She reached up and pushed her hair back, knocking loose some leaves and a twig. "Visibility is near zero, and there's a lot of debris swirling around."

"I need to check with the weather service again. I hadn't realized the clouds were so low." Meg shook her head as she leaned over to read from the clipboard the mayor was once again holding. "There's a timeline to what we'll experience, and it gives us a decent indication of how far off the leading edge is to making landfall. We need to get moving *now*. With your staff of four directing traffic, you won't have anyone to spare 'til after most folks are gone."

"Four? You're including Greg?"

"He's a trained crossing guard. As am I. I'll take the northeast point here." She pointed to a spot where all the north-south roads funneled together before turning toward the bridge. "He can take the northwest one here. The other four of you—"

Rebecca raised a hand. "I've got someone detained at the station. I can't leave him unattended."

"Let him go." The mayor shook his head. "Whatever he did, he can be picked up for later."

"He may have brutally murdered a woman in her

bedroom sometime last night." Rebecca tried to keep her words polite, but her tone made it clear this was not up for debate. "I lost count of the stab wounds."

Mayor Doughtie and Meg both stared at her while she finally poured herself a fresh cup of steaming coffee.

"Murder? You're working a case?"

Rebecca nodded her response to the mayor's question as she sipped at her steaming cup.

"Good lord," the mayor breathed while Meg turned to glare at Vale.

Rebecca followed her gaze. "I take it Mr. Vale didn't tell you where I was."

Doughtie's nostrils flared. "No, he did not."

Meg put her hand on Rebecca's arm. "That means you'll be down one more person. Have you secured the scene yet?"

"That's what I was attempting to do when I was called here. Deputy Frost is there working on that now. But he's working alone, so it will take time. Paramedics are removing the remains."

Doughtie looked at Meg, and she gave him a twisted frown. Rebecca understood why he was checking with Meg. She had been a police dispatcher for most of her life and knew more about what it involved than any civilian.

"That complicates things. Can you even secure the scene in this?" She gestured vaguely at the walls and roof being hammered by the storm.

"I've never tried to work through a hurricane. I have no idea. We're following what the forensic team told us to do, sealing each door. But Hoyt pointed out that if the windows don't hold, it won't matter. So we're taking as much digital proof as we can, which is hard with only one person on the scene." Rebecca remembered the radios in her pockets and set down her coffee. "I brought these to give to the volunteer leaders. Meg, you should definitely have one if you don't already. I'll let you decide who else gets one."

"Good thinking, hun. We're likely to lose electricity soon, and we'll need a way to stay in touch."

"Exactly. You can still coordinate routine communications through dispatch. But if there's an emergency, use the radio."

Meg offered a mock salute and a smile as bright as her daughter's. "Roger that."

"All right, let's put everyone you can on traffic." Mayor Doughtie pushed forward as he scooped up a radio for himself, though Rebecca doubted Meg would let him keep it. "I know you're running tight with personnel, though I can't understand why. Let's get people to safety first, then deal with your staffing issues after things have settled down."

If it ever settles down.

"HEY, Boss, how did the meeting go?" Viviane leaned over the reception desk to beam at her.

Rebecca struggled to get her soaked raincoat off. "I need to speak to everyone." She finally managed to get her arms out of the clinging sleeves. She left the coat turned inside out, hoping the interior would dry a little before she had to put it on again. "Can you ask everyone to meet in the bullpen?"

"No problem." Instead of calling each deputy, she cupped her hands around her mouth and shouted. "Everyone gather for a meeting." She faced Rebecca again. "Do you need Angie? She's in the bathroom, I think."

Did she? Probably, but Angie Frost was officially a civilian.

"Just the staff right now. That includes you too."

Viviane groaned. "Oh, this can't be good."

She hopped down from her chair and followed Rebecca into the bullpen, where the rest of the staff had already gathered. Darian stood next to the coffee maker, a steaming cup in his hand while Greg leaned back in his chair against the wall. Deputy Trent Locke glowered from the far wall. His pant legs were soaked, so he hadn't been there for long.

Rebecca blew out her breath as she took in her meager force.

"I just came from town hall, where they voted to ask the governor for disaster assistance and push for mandatory evacuation. We need to facilitate the evacuation efforts and do so as quickly and smoothly as possible. The roads are already getting crowded, as I'm sure you've noticed. We're going with plan A."

Locke snorted, puffing out his already beefy chest. "Did Hoyt tell you to use that one, or are you just picking the first your eyeballs landed on?"

Rebecca turned to meet his glare. A dozen heartbeats later, he dropped his gaze to his boots.

"Hoyt and I agreed." She turned her attention back to the three who hadn't spoken. Locke said it, but Rebecca had been worrying about the decision the entire drive over, especially when she'd seen a fish flopping about on the road. With a shrug to hide her discomfort, she continued. "I'm an investigator. I've never been a traffic cop or a patrol officer. Even worse, I know little about local traffic patterns or what a hurricane might throw at us. Figuratively or literally. I plowed through as much of the emergency binder as I could, but I'm out of my depth here. Any suggestions are appreciated."

"Go ahead and sound the siren right away," Viviane offered, "so people will know we're coming. We need to change the evacuation from voluntary to mandatory."

Rebecca's eyes widened. "Now? Shouldn't we make sure

we're at our assigned positions first? Wait for the mayor to confirm?"

Viviane crossed her arms over her ample chest. "Yeah. Tell us what you want us to do."

I have no idea.

She turned to Greg, knowing desperation was clear on her face. She didn't care. Now wasn't the time for ego or pride.

Darian and Greg shared a long look that was full of silent communication. Greg sighed and pushed to his feet. "Do you mind?"

Rebecca shook her head and waved at him to continue, paying attention to everything he said. "The floor is yours."

Greg gave a stiff-necked nod. "Darian, you're at the bridge entrance. Locke and I will take the corners of Main Street and Coastal Drive to help guide traffic toward the bridge and keep it moving in the same direction. You've already weighed down the vehicles, right, Locke?"

Locke froze like a deer in headlights. "I…"

Greg's usually cheery face darkened. "Locke?"

Locke lifted a shoulder. "I got most of them, but Darian called me back in and…"

Greg's hands clenched at his sides, and he raised his eyes to the ceiling, as if seeking divine intervention.

Before he could say whatever he was going to say, Rebecca stepped in. "Take the heaviest one we have and get to your station."

Greg wouldn't be put off. "Follow the evacuation route to a T, boy. Do not fuck this up too. You'll get dozens of people killed if you do. Keep an eye on the breakers around us. The waves are getting really high already."

Rebecca jumped back into the fray. "Don't any of you get caught in one of them. Keep your radios on at all times and keep an eye on the batteries. Watch your backs and your feet.

Reflective gear and flashlights the whole time, but no sirens. No one can hear us, so we must make sure they see us. And make sure no one comes onto the island. They shouldn't be able to. Coastal Ridge PD will be keeping everyone off the bridge. No one in, everyone out. You got it?"

"Yes, ma'am." Locke darted off like his ass was on fire.

"Good job, Sheriff. You handle what you know best, and we'll handle what we know. No offense, ma'am." Greg dug through his desk drawer while the others hurried off to take their positions, which they'd apparently drilled for before Rebecca had ever come to the island.

"None taken. This takes a load of worry off my shoulders. Thanks for jumping in."

"That's what support staff is for, ma'am." He pulled a folder from his drawer along with an oversized reflective vest. Handing her the folder, he headed for the door. "I've kept notes over the years that wouldn't have been in that binder you read. They'll tell you everything you need to know."

Her pager buzzed and she glanced at the screen. *Evac approved.*

"Looks like mandatory evacuation is a go." Rebecca took the folder with a nod. "How long will you need before we turn on the sirens?"

"Go ahead and do it now. We'll be at our positions before residents can even get in their cars. And tell Hoyt that, once he's loose, to take up his position. He knows where he belongs. Take care of that murder, and I'll radio if we need your boots on the ground." He swung the door closed with a violent slam. The wind was getting even worse.

Rebecca blew out a long breath. "Speaking of, I still need to track down the victim's next of kin, Brady Munroe. Viviane, can you find his number for me while I go deal with the rest of this?"

Viviane lifted an eyebrow. "Before or after we turn on the siren?"

Shit.

"After."

Viviane held out her hand. "Gimme your keys."

Rebecca handed them over, trusting Viviane knew what she was doing.

Viviane walked over to a panel next to the bulletin board on the wall behind reception. Rebecca followed. Using the keys, her dispatcher unlocked the door and opened it. There was an array of switches. Each one was marked, but she didn't have time to read them.

Viviane pulled out an unusually shaped key, which she showed to Rebecca, unlocked one of the switches, and pressed it.

Outside, the unmistakable wail of sirens rang out.

"Done." Viviane closed the panel and handed the keys back to Rebecca. "They'll run for thirty minutes. Sound them again when we do the second sweep to check for stragglers."

Rebecca wondered how Viviane knew exactly what to do but didn't question it.

"Thank you."

"Sure thing." She gave Rebecca a salute and headed for her desk. Rebecca smiled at the similarity in mannerisms between mother and daughter. "I'll search for Brady Munroe's contact information right after I ring the mayor and let him know our guys are moving into position."

Emotion burned Rebecca's eyes, but she blinked any sign of weakness away. "Good thinking, and thanks again."

Viviane was on the phone already, and Rebecca listened as she informed the mayor of their next steps.

"Well, you guys sure know how to scare it out of a girl." Angie chuckled as she walked back into the bullpen. "You're lucky I didn't make a mess all over the floor when that siren sounded."

Rebecca laughed. "Sorry about that. The decision was just made. We contacted the governor for assistance, and the evacuation has turned mandatory. The hurricane is gaining force."

"Oh, well then. I guess I need to start making phone calls and get to packing. Don't you worry, Sheriff, we'll make sure you all don't go hungry." Angie took her seat at her husband's desk, pulled out her phone, and began typing.

In the sudden silence, the fury of the storm grew louder.

Closer.

Bearing down like a monster ready to eat them alive.

10

Hoyt pulled into the Shadow Island Community Health Center parking lot right behind the rocking ambulance. The driver knew what he was doing but driving such a big, boxy vehicle in these winds wasn't easy.

He looped the cruiser around as the ambulance turned and started backing up to the side entrance, angling to get as much protection from the wind as possible while still allowing enough room to open the doors.

Hoyt had a vehicle full of evidence and two memory cards filled with pictures and videos. The lighting had been terrible as the electricity kept flickering on and off, but he believed it would all still be usable.

The main thing he had to worry about was getting the body bag and all its contents safely into the building. They'd learned, trying to carry Clare out of the house, that the thick plastic caught the wind and made even holding onto it a struggle.

Parking next to the ambulance, he jumped out and ran over to give as much help as he could. Baker was already on the ground, holding the bag as her partner lowered it.

Someone from inside had the door open. The emergency staff were wearing scrubs and gowns, ready to try and save a life. None of them were wearing coats. And all of them were staring at the body bag.

Did they think we were bringing a patient?

The call had kept breaking up, and he'd learned the hard way that this place wasn't retrofitted with radios in every department.

"Grab the bag!" Sandra screamed, her feet sliding in the torrent of water shooting from the downspouts.

Trying to be mindful of the barbed wire, Hoyt wrapped his arm around where he guessed the victim's waist would be. His whispered apology to Clare was carried away by the wind as he pushed to keep her from being torn out of their hands.

"Don't!" Sandra screamed.

One of the nurses had darted over to help them and was about to grab the legs the same way he had.

"Punctures!" her yell was all the warning she was able to get out as she struggled with the bag.

The nurse froze, stared at the boxy, strangely shaped bag, then nodded and joined Sandra at the feet. Both women hauled on the hand straps. With the four of them working together, they were finally able to get through the door safely.

"This isn't what we were expecting, but we have a room ready." The nurse who had held the door open for them pointed toward a hallway.

The one who had helped get them through the door stepped back, now that she wasn't needed, and pulled the soaked paper mask off her face. "I'll show you where."

She led the way down the hall and opened a door, waving them inside. Now that they were out of the wind, it was easy enough for the two paramedics to lift the body onto the table. Hoyt followed them, stepping to the side so he was out of their way.

"Thank you, Nurse..." Her badge was flipped over, hiding her name from Hoyt's sight.

"Missy. Just call me Missy." Her gaze was glued to the strange shape of the bag that was even more evident now that it was laid out on the table. "I'll let Dr. Evan know about this...change of plans."

"And let her know we need her to sign off, too, please." Kendric looked over to Hoyt. "We need to get back out there. There's plenty for us to do. Already got three incidents lined up."

"You going to need me for any of those?" He asked out of professionalism, but hoped the answer was no.

Kendric shook his head. "Two falls and a panic attack. All at residences. We'll be good."

While waiting for the doctor to show up, the two paramedics availed themselves of the facilities, getting cleaned up and dried off as much as possible.

Hoyt stayed in the room with his arms crossed over his chest. Countless meaningless conversations raced through his mind.

Angie and Clare talking about *The Notebook,* laughing about starting their own sisterhood and traveling. Clare mentioning how she had always wanted children, but the Munroes' busy work schedules had buried that dream.

Buried. It's all gone. Why? Why, Clare? Who did this to you?

His memories were interrupted by the door opening, followed immediately by a harried-looking doctor.

"Morning, all. I'm Dr. Evan. I hear I'm not needed for the usual reasons. What's going on?"

Both paramedics pointed to Hoyt.

He stepped forward, holding his hands out. "Sorry about the miscommunication, Doc. I tried to let them know what I was asking for, but there was a problem with the phones."

"Same problem we're having with everything else, I'm sure."

"We've got a corpse. I've identified her already. But we can't get her to the forensic center because of the storm, so we had to bring her here."

"I get that. But what do you need from me right now? I've just revived a teenage boy who thought it was a good time to surf. Damn fool nearly drowned."

What's wrong with people?

"We need you to sign for the body and give us a place to store her."

"Signature is fine." She took the clipboard from Sandra. "Exam rooms are all filled up. We're actually diverting as many as possible. We're triaging cases as they arrive."

"Is there anywhere else on the island that will be safe enough to secure a body?"

The doctor was already shaking her head. "We've got cold storage. That's the best I can do. She can't sit here like this. Decomposition should already be setting in."

She set the papers down and opened the body bag without signing them. Her lips clamped together, and she leaned back as the knife in the chest was exposed. Gathering her composure, she continued to unzip the bag. Her eyes flinched as she revealed the bloody sheets wrapped around the macabre mermaid tail.

"This is horrendous." Even though Clare was clearly dead, the doctor pressed two fingers to her neck before signing the forms.

With their duties fulfilled, the paramedics took their leave. The shrill blast of the hurricane siren echoed through the tiled halls when they opened the doors.

Dr. Evan turned to Hoyt. "Deputy, are we evacuating?"

"Sounds like it." He grabbed his radio and clicked the mic, but nothing happened. Looking down, he saw that it must have been turned off when he was struggling outside.

No wonder there's been no radio chatter.

Turning it on, Rebecca's voice came through. "Again, if you can hear me, Deputy Frost, respond immediately. Over."

Cursing silently that she'd been trying to get ahold of him for a while, Hoyt answered. "Boss, this is Frost. Over."

"Forget to turn your radio on this morning? Over." Her chuckle was cut off as she released the microphone key.

"Copy that, but I didn't forget. It must have gotten tangled up while I was working. You got me out here doing all the heavy lifting while you sit back and enjoy my wife's cooking. I have my ears on now. Sounds like we're evacuating. Over."

Every eye was on him, and he reminded himself to keep it professional.

"We are. Over."

As soon as Rebecca had answered, the nurses and doctors around Hoyt scattered into a frenzied scuffle.

"Triage everyone still waiting. If they're ambulatory, send them to Coastal Ridge Hospital. Denise, get rooms eight and eleven prepped for transfer. Jill, go check the generator and make sure it's ready to go." Dr. Evan marched away, shouting orders nonstop.

Everyone started talking loud and fast, all at once. Patients and their families came wandering over to see what was going on.

Hoyt missed everything else Rebecca said. "Ten-one, Boss. We just kicked up a hornet's nest here. Let me get somewhere quiet and out of their way. Over."

"Copy that. Over."

Taking long strides and dodging medical staff, Hoyt made

his way back to the exam room where he'd left Clare. Closing the door, he was finally able to hear again.

"Okay, Boss. Please repeat. Over."

"I said, can anyone there do a visual inspection of the body? We need to collect any evidence we can. Over."

"My guess is no one has the time to do that, considering how much they're all running around out there. They've got a lot of people in here. And now they have to get them to safety. Over."

There was a long pause before Rebecca's tired voice responded. "Roger. Okay. I'll be there as soon as I can. You're needed to help with traffic for the evac, but I need to know what else you found at the scene. Wait for me there and keep your ears on. I'm going to need help. If they're all busy, it looks like it will just be you and me. Over."

Hoyt did not want to think about what that could mean and swallowed hard.

"I'll be waiting." He took a deep breath and realized he couldn't hold himself back anymore. "Boss, is my wife there? Over."

"She is. She mentioned you'd ask about her second because you're a good cop first. Over."

Angie's voice came over the line. "I love you, sweetheart."

Hoyt's entire body relaxed, hearing his wife was safe.

"I've got Boomer, and we're about to head off the island. I dropped off more food at the town hall and alerted my mother, so she knows we're coming. I also let the boys know about the evac, so they won't worry."

"Good thinking."

"Well," the smile in her voice was clear, "one of us needs to think with their big head, you know."

He chuckled. Damn, he loved his wife. "You are correct."

"You take care of yourself and join us when you can. And

make sure you change your socks. I'm sure they're wet." She was rambling now.

"I love you too, dear."

He almost added "over," but the word got stuck in his throat.

Over felt a little too literal today.

11

Walking into the health center was nearly as tricky as keeping her feet under her in the parking lot.

Streams of people pushed past Rebecca, some heading for their cars while others sought treatment. There'd already been a scattered number of vehicles leaving the area. Unfortunately, not all of them had headed directly for the bridge. Others had turned toward the residential areas.

In her head, she knew these were people who had been here for a while, probably hours, considering how many of them were leaving. They needed to go home to collect belongings or the rest of their family. But in her heart, she wanted to see every car on this island pointed toward safety.

The fish swimming through the middle of town had pushed her past the limits of what she thought she knew as reality. Now there was seaweed in the trees. In the damn trees.

Next, it'll start raining frogs. Oh, dear God, why did I even think that? Of course it's going to start raining frogs now. It's already raining fish and kelp!

Flashing her badge at a staff member got her the answer to where Hoyt was waiting with the murder victim.

Hoyt jumped as she walked into the exam room when the evidence kit she was lugging bounced loudly off the door-frame as she tried to maneuver it, along with two empty buckets. His face was pale, and she couldn't tell if he was sweating or if his hair was still dripping from the rain.

Poor guy. He doesn't deal well with dead bodies at the best of times. And knowing the victim has to make this even harder.

"Fill me in." Rebecca gave him something else to focus on while she peeled off her stuffy coat and started reading labels on the doors and drawers.

"I did as you ordered. The rooms are taped up. I did a full walk-through before and after. Found these." He dug around in his pocket and pulled out an evidence bag containing a key ring with only two keys and a car fob.

"Well, that complicates matters even more." Rebecca sighed, finally finding the drawers she needed and setting out tools on a tray.

"How so?" Hoyt's eyes were laser-focused on the tray she was assembling.

"Those are Brady Munroe's keys. Not Clare's."

Hoyt flipped the bag around and stared at it. "How can you tell?"

"She drives a BMW. That's for a Lexus."

"Maybe they switched cars? Or he left his keys at home? He could have gotten a ride to the airport."

"Why do you think he went to the airport?"

"They have a calendar in their kitchen. He was supposed to take the red-eye out last night and be gone for a week."

Rebecca pondered that as she moved to the sink and washed her hands up to her wrists.

"Uh, Boss, what are you planning on doing with all that stuff?"

"We can't get to the M.E.'s. Before this body decomposes further, I need some information, so I'm going to do a preliminary search."

"Can you do that? I mean, legally speaking, uh, we did already get permission to move the body, but, uh, don't you think Bailey is going to be pissed if you start..." He gulped hard.

"Geez, Hoyt, I'm not going to cut into her. I'm only going to take a closer look now that we're in a sterile environment and I don't have to worry about mucking up the scene."

"Oh. Okay. But what did you want me to do?"

"Just hold the bag open. You're not trained anyway."

"And you are?"

"I might have spent an awful lot of time at the body farm. I was getting some extra certifications."

"The...what?"

"Forensic Anthropology Center in Knoxville. They call it the Body Farm 'cause it looks like a farm. Except with mostly buried remains in different conditions and stages."

"Oh, that sounds like a lovely place to vacation in the summer."

Rebecca pulled on two sets of gloves. "It wasn't bad. Not that I slept over there or anything. I got a hotel in town. Traveled back during the day." She propped up her phone on a nearby tray and recorded everything she was doing.

"So, how did your meeting with Vale go?"

"Surprisingly well. He was an overbearing jerk, as you'd expect. Meg and the mayor were there too. They kept things moving along. We went with plan A."

"Isn't all this a bit early? I thought we still had several hours or so."

Rebecca glanced over at him. "You haven't heard the latest news?"

Hoyt's face went stony. "I've been working the crime

scene. How could I hear anything?" He blew out a breath and sucked in a fresh one. Then he waved his hand in a go-ahead motion. "Okay, I'm ready. What's the new timeline?"

"Less than nine hours 'til landfall."

He ran a hand through his hair. "That fast?"

"Yeah, so we need to get things moving as quickly as possible."

"And hope this building holds up."

She glanced at the heavy cinder block walls. "Seriously? This place is built like a fortress. You think the hurricane will be that strong?"

"That strong?" Hoyt's jaw dropped. "West, think of the biggest tornado you've ever heard of or seen. Now add water, fish, and maybe a couple of boats. That's a hurricane. That's what's about to hit us."

She groaned. "It's going to start raining frogs, isn't it?"

Hoyt laughed, a light barking sound. "That's not impossible, honestly. It's happened before with regular storms."

Vaguely remembering a Bible story about gaining protection from God's wrath, she joked, "And I forgot to paint the doorframe before I left home today." Trying to ignore the dread building up in her stomach, Rebecca carefully peeled a piece of seaweed from the victim's hair. "This looks like the same kind we'd find on the shore. What do you think?"

She passed over the bag she'd dropped it in.

Hoyt carefully moved it around, inspecting it through the clear plastic. "Yup. It looks like every other bit of seagrass I've ever seen. Yellow and orange with blobs on it. Smells bad." He pointed at the other piece she was trying to work free of Clare's hair. "And that red stuff. It only comes up on fishing lines or during a storm."

"During a storm. Like now." Rebecca turned to face her phone, which was recording, and held up the floppy piece she'd been working on. "Which could mean this was harvested recently and then placed on the body."

He nodded. "Very possible."

"Which also could mean those pieces, along with the parts wrapped around her legs, were newly gathered. But the hair, makeup, fabric mermaid tail, and the painted seashells seem planned." Rebecca examined the embedded blade. "So she dressed herself up as a pretty mermaid, and someone killed her and destroyed whatever she had planned?"

"Maybe."

Hoyt's tone was filled with so much devastation, she glanced over.

He was still staring at the bag in his hands.

Rebecca stopped the recording. "Hoyt." She had to wait a few moments before she got his attention. "If this is hitting home too much, you can wait outside."

His eyes widened, and she thought he would take her up on the offer. "No. I'm fine." He crossed his arms over his chest and locked eyes with her.

She knew he was lying through his teeth. "In that case, I need you to find a picture from the kitchen that shows the knife block. I saw it on my way out but didn't get a good look."

"I can do that." Hoyt nodded and patted his pockets. "It's…I left the camera in the cruiser."

"Okay, well, go get it. Oh, and grab a couple radios out of my cruiser and give one to whoever's in charge. We need to make sure these folks have plenty of them."

"Yeah, I can do that."

Rebecca let out a sigh of relief as the door closed behind him. She understood where he was coming from. Most people weren't comfortable around dead bodies, let alone friends who had been killed in such a disturbing manner.

Now that Hoyt was out of the room, she resumed the

recording and tilted the body over to check the back side. The growing rigor mortis made the job easier.

She'd only just ducked her head down to inspect the back when the door opened again. Peeking over her shoulder, she expected to see Hoyt.

Instead, it was a woman with a tight braid wrapped around her head, wearing a white lab coat. She glared at her.

"Excuse me. What exactly do you think you're doing?"

Rebecca respectfully lowered the corpse and raised her hands. She twisted to the side, hoping her badge was visible on her belt. "Sorry, I must have missed you in the madness out there. I'm Sheriff West, this is my case, and I'm examining the body while collecting evidence."

The doctor's eyes narrowed. "I can't see your badge."

Rebecca stripped off her gloves and pulled it out with a sigh.

The doctor relaxed and walked the rest of the way into the room. She held her hand out to shake. "Sorry, but bad weather brings out the weirdos. I'm Dr. Evan."

"Good to meet you, even if the circumstances are so grim. I don't even want to know the kind of crazy you see in these halls." Rebecca laughed and turned to wash her hands once more.

"But what are you doing? Exact details, please. I've signed for this body, so it's my ass on the line if you do something." She inspected the corpse intently.

"Not much to the body itself. I know my limits. I'm really worried about the hurricane and if the M.E. will have a body to examine once Boris passes. Believe me when I say I'd never do this if there weren't extenuating circumstances. I'm simply collecting the evidence that was brought in with the body as we rushed from the scene." Now that she was gloved up, she rolled the body again. "I'd noticed holes in the bed, and I thought some were punch-throughs."

"Need a hand?" Dr. Evan washed her hands and then pulled on gloves without waiting for an answer.

"If you wouldn't mind. My deputy is a bit squeamish, and he knows the vic."

"Right, Clare and Angie were friends." Dr. Evan braced the body on its side, so the back wasn't hidden in shadows.

Rebecca spotted at least five exit wounds crusted with blood.

"Did you know the victim too?"

"Not really. I know her face and her first name. I wasn't sure of her last name until I signed the paperwork. But I've seen her and Angie at lunch a few times, and I know they talked about movies often. They're both hopeless romantics." She frowned at the body she was holding. "Or she was."

"I didn't know she and Angie were so well acquainted. This has to be hard on Hoyt, then." Rebecca frowned. Just like Angie had said, Hoyt was a good cop. He'd swallowed his pain and done his job. "Can you help me?"

"What do you need?"

"I need to take measurements."

Dr. Evan nodded. "Of the stab wounds?"

Rebecca nodded as they set the body back down.

"Before he gets back?"

"Preferably."

She indicated the knife. "Let's be quick so he doesn't have to look at this."

12

The world had been washed away in a haze of gray. The blue of the sky, and the gold of the sun, had both been replaced by swirls of gray. The pink of her lips, purple on her chest, green of her eyes. The scarlet of her blood. It was all covered. Blanketed. Hidden. It was all gone.

Everything was gray. The world had lost its vibrancy. Now whatever I looked at was flat, dull, and bland.

A constant noise covered everything. I couldn't tell if it was real or just in my head. It was this steady pounding that seemed to rock my entire body.

Did I have a headache? Had I hit my head? I tried to run my hands over my aching scalp to feel if something was wrong. But I was so tired. My strength had been leeched away the same way my color had.

What's wrong with me? Did something happen? Something that left the world so empty and lifeless?

I couldn't remember. Not what caused this, not even when it started or what was real before this new reality. I shook my head, trying to clear it. As if that would help me remember.

But the pounding was still there. It was just so very loud.

I could actually feel it pulsating through my skin. I couldn't get away from it. I was so tired. Everything ached.

And all I could hear was the pounding. There wasn't even a rhythm to the noise. Was there more to the world around me outside this arhythmic torture?

The sound of birds? The sound of cars? I thought I remembered those. The sound of another voice? I opened my mouth to speak but couldn't tell if I'd succeeded. I couldn't hear anything over the droning.

Except…my hands. I *could* feel something with my hands. I wiggled my fingers, trying to figure out what it was.

It had a smooth grain, like sanded wood. Evenly spaced circles were set inside the smooth wood. One side of it had curves. The other was straight. My fingers wrapped around it so easily. I tried to look down to see what it was that my hands clasped, but all was gray.

Was I lost in a dense fog? That could explain it. A fog so thick I couldn't even see my body. A fog so heavy, the mist wrapped around me like a wet blanket.

That idea made sense. I was less worried now.

My fingers slipped. I touched warmth. That was a new sensation.

I looked down at my hands. At ruby red lining my fingernails.

That wasn't right. How could I see color? How could I see my hands if they were wrapped in a thick fog?

No. Everything is gray.

Everything *had* to be gray, so I wouldn't see it.

I couldn't see it.

Clare's smiling face. Her green eyes dancing as she looked at me—the golden flecks in the emerald that only I could see.

That wasn't right either. Everything was gray. Everything was supposed to be gray and muted and dull.

And Clare wasn't smiling. She was…grimacing. Why? Why was she looking at me like that? Was she in pain?

Her soft pink lipstick was smeared. Was it from my kisses, as it had been so many times before?

I wanted to reach out. To fix it for her. She hated when her makeup wasn't perfect. I could make this right. I could fix it. Then she wouldn't look at me that way anymore. She would smile at me instead.

But my hands wouldn't move.

I looked down at them. The fog lifted, and I could see them more clearly now.

They were clenched so tight they hurt. My knuckles were white from the strain, splattered with drips of red, and wrapped around the handle of a knife.

The knife that was buried in her chest. In me. Buried in a brilliant bloom of red. Why was there red on her chest? On mine?

"Anemone." Yes. That's what it had to be. It was a vivid, cherry red sea anemone that was laid on her chest. That made so much more sense. It was a present for her. "For my mermaid."

She deserves only the very best. She loves flowers. And bright, happy colors.

I remembered her face the first time I brought her a beautiful bouquet. Back when the world still had color and sound…and life.

It was on our second date. She was so happy to get them. I'd bought her a bouquet of carnations and daffodils, with those tiny white flowers and greenery woven around it. The florist had wrapped them up after placing each flower just right, so their colors blended.

Clare's eyes lit up as she took them and held them to her nose. She bathed her face in the colors I gave her and reveled in the fragrance.

Their colors were washed away now, like everything else. Swept away like the tide. Only gray remained.

I remembered the last time I gave her flowers. It had been an enormous bouquet of red roses in a crystal vase. I'd bought them at a grocery store instead of a florist, but they'd been nice. They'd been so heavy. She accepted them. But there was no smile.

Why?

Why did I get her roses if they didn't make her smile?

The fight.

I'd bought them to apologize. She accepted my apology. Because she loved me. Her arms wrapped me in a tight embrace. She didn't revel in the flowers or bury herself in them. But she did cling to me.

I held her in my blood-covered hands. The world was splattered in color. In vibrant crimson hues. Even the carpet squelched with color as I moved. Blood bubbled up from it. Blood dripped down onto it. Blood covered everything. Nothing was gray.

No.

No.

No.

She deserves only the best things. My mermaid. Mine! My beautiful siren.

"What have I done?" The sound was loud coming out of my mouth. Louder than the noise on my skin. I stared at it. My gray skin. Gray like a corpse.

No.

I'm not a corpse. I can make this right.

"What have I done?" How did my voice become so strong? Louder than the pounding from before.

Yes. Strike after strike. Each strike made it hurt less. I did it again and felt better. I kept doing it. Up, down, up. The motion made it all fade away. The pain ebbed.

The first time, I didn't even feel the resistance. Or the second. The third was soft. The fourth...was loud. How could it be noisy? This was supposed to make everything better. Not worse.

I struck again to make the pain stop. To end what hurt me. To make sure it never hurt me again.

Would it wash away? On a tide of red?

I stared at the wall with the red handprint. From my red hand. I brushed it away. Tried to wipe it out. Everything should be gray. Not red.

This wasn't right. This wasn't helping!

Everything faded to gray once more, and I could think again. The pain had stopped.

I had to do something. I had to make this right.

The handle of the knife was warm in my hands. Not as warm as the gray liquid that splashed over it.

She liked bright, vibrant colors.

If I gave her those things, she'd stay with me.

My lover. My everything. My mermaid...mine!

The wind howled. It was the storm. It had to be the storm that was screaming. Not my siren. She would never scream like that. She could never make that terrible noise.

Her mouth was open wide. All the pink was gone. Masked by the red that had hidden it. Her cold gray eyes stared at me.

With love? I knew she loved me. I could prove my love to her. Show her how much I loved her. Prove how much she meant to me. Show her...what it meant to be an actual mythical mermaid—a vibrant, seductive, creature of the sea.

The wind was screaming. The pounding on my skin grew stronger. I closed my eyes.

13

It was bad enough that Clare had been brutally killed, but then her corpse had been posed and decorated, dehumanizing her further. Out of respect for her, Rebecca and Dr. Evan had worked methodically and carefully. Preserving the evidence was paramount, but they also wanted to respect the victim.

Although Rebecca wanted to fingerprint the knife's wooden handle, the risk of further contaminating the body wasn't worth it. She decided leaving it in place might provide Bailey with vital information that could help her case. Likewise, the medical examiner would be able to measure internally the depth of the wounds and angle of attack to determine the positioning of the killer.

Dr. Evan and Rebecca managed to get most of the stabs measured, and they checked the edges of the wounds before Hoyt got back to the room. Rebecca had asked for the blood around the final stab wound to be collected. The health center didn't have advanced testing available, but they could still perform typing. Rebecca hoped that would be enough for what she needed.

By the time her senior deputy returned, they had the body covered in a white sheet so he wouldn't have to see her any longer. It was the least they could do for him.

All the stab wounds were consistent in size to have been caused by the single knife embedded in Clare's chest. Dr. Evan's visual inspection revealed the last blow had more than likely severed a major artery. Its location and the volume of blood pooled around that wound were consistent with that finding. It would take a complete autopsy to verify, but it appeared she'd bled out.

While her hands were tied by the absence of an autopsy, Rebecca hoped she'd gathered enough information for now.

After handing out additional radios to the staff, Rebecca and Hoyt headed out. He needed to get to his position controlling traffic, and the evidence still needed to be secured. It wouldn't make sense for them to have gone through so much to collect it only to lose it on a flooded road.

As it was, the back half of the parking lot at the station was already flooding when Rebecca arrived in the cruiser. Over where she'd parked her truck that morning, water had risen halfway up the tires, and she tried not to dwell on the ramifications of that.

"She's safer here than she would be at the beach house, at least." Even spoken out loud, the assurance didn't do much to ease her anxiety about her truck's well-being. Instead, she promised herself she would take her girl in for a complete checkup as soon as this was done. Heck, with all the debris, it would probably need a good detailing too.

If there was anything left.

Viviane was on the phone when she entered. "Yes, ma'am, we're asking all residents to evacuate as soon as possible. No, ma'am. Yes, ma'am. Yes, ma'am. Of course, over the bridge.

Just follow the signs and the emergency personnel. Yes, ma'am. Drive safe now."

When Viviane disconnected the call, Rebecca wrinkled her nose. "Has it been bad?"

"This phone has been ringing off the hook. Why can't people understand to turn on the radio and follow directions? That's why we have the damn sirens! Why do they have to call in and make me repeat everything that's already been said?"

"Fear can make people stupid."

Yet another reason they needed a town-wide review of evacuation protocols as soon as Boris blew over.

Viviane slapped the reception desk. "I just had a woman ask if she should take the bridge. The bridge! How the heck does she think she's getting off the island otherwise?"

The phone rang again, and Viviane groaned.

"Set up an auto-response with all the evacuation information," Rebecca suggested. "That can answer first, then transfer to your phone if they stay on the line."

Viviane palmed her face. "Why the heck didn't I think of that? And I can route any unanswered calls to the main. I just need to find the manual to remember how."

Rebecca examined the antiquated equipment and wondered how hard it would be to get them set up with a computerized system. "Sometimes we can't see the forest for the trees."

"Oh, and I found Brady Munroe's number. It's in the file whenever you need it. I did try calling him earlier but got no answer. His voicemail was full, so I couldn't leave a message."

Rebecca massaged her temples. "How's Mr. Jenner doing?"

"Darian and Greg were adamant about not entering the interrogation room alone. He's not cuffed, but the door is closed. I've peeked at him through the viewing pane twice, and he just stares at the wall. It's like he's catatonic."

"Right. I don't want you in there. He's unstable. Until we have a better idea what we're dealing with, best to be careful." As Rebecca raised her head, a red light caught her eye. A slow cooker was warming on the counter. And another one on the table. There was a third on Hoyt's desk.

"Are those from Angie?"

Viviane shook her head. "Mama and the others evacuated as ordered, but they dropped these off first. Left even more over at the shelter at the town hall." Viviane spun around in the chair to grin at her. "Make sure you try Mama's chili. Cornbread's in the plastic container in the corner."

A container with a faded label that read *Darby*.

"I know it's morning, but chili sounds pretty damn good. I love this town."

Rebecca poured herself a cup of chili and added a piece of cornbread to go with it. Her fitness tracking watch indicated it was just after eight thirty. Amazing how disorienting the time of day was without the rising and setting of the sun.

How do people in Alaska and Iceland manage without daylight for part of the year?

As she savored the hot food in her new office chair, she used the time to scroll through Malcolm Jenner's phone. What she found was spicier than the chili.

He'd been having a year-long affair with Clare Munroe. All of it was scheduled around Brady's work trips. From the look of it, Brady was gone more days than he was home. There'd been plenty of time for a relationship to bloom.

It wasn't just physical. They were in love.

Or he was just saying that to keep her interested?

She scrolled all the way back to the very first message Clare had sent him. It had been to ask about a product his pharmaceutical company manufactured. His response had been politely professional, but after a few weeks, it became friendly.

It went on for months with just a few texts each week. There were jumps where it looked like they were talking about things they'd done together in person, but nothing that was salacious. Earlier messages discussed dance classes they were taking. Apparently, Clare had needed a partner.

She checked other gaps in their texting against the family calendar Hoyt had taken from the scene. Clare's business travel aligned with those gaps.

In one text, Malcolm told her about his mother, who had recently passed. She mentioned how the only family she had was her husband, and how much she loved him. They even compared dating horror stories and plans for their own individual futures. Clare was going to surprise her husband with her newly acquired dancing skills, and Malcolm was saving money for the trip of a lifetime.

Picking up a different calendar Hoyt confiscated, Rebecca noticed that, about a year ago, one of Clare's business trips coincided with when she asked if she could meet Malcolm in private. She'd just learned something about her marriage, and she needed a friend she could talk to. The next one after that was Clare apologizing for kissing him. She'd been overwhelmed after learning her husband was a serial cheater, and Brady had been unfazed when she'd confronted him.

Malcolm apologized for letting the kiss happen. The man was either a very patient smooth talker, or he really had feelings for her.

There was a long string of brief messages, simply checking to make sure the other person had gotten home safely, indicating they were meeting in person more often than not. Then she went on another business trip and texted him every night and day.

On her return to the island, things started getting intimate. There was a slew of pictures sent back and forth with just as revealing text messages—more than Rebecca wanted to see. Mixed in with more mundane messages were declarations of love and their shared desire to be together again soon.

It was a blazing romance. The very last message Clare had sent promised Malcolm a special sexy outfit on their next encounter.

Rebecca pressed back into the padded luxury of her chair. *If Angie and Clare were close, why didn't Clare turn to her when she was in need of a friend?* Was there something else going on beyond what these messages implied?

Rebecca collected Jenner's phone and her notes and headed to the locked interrogation room where he was being held. It wasn't the ideal place to hold him during a natural disaster, but the sheriff's office sometimes served as an overflow shelter when the town hall became too crowded. Greg's notes had shed light on that detail, which the binder never addressed.

Jenner was still sitting in his chair, seemingly unaware of anything around him. The blanket had fallen off his shoulders and was hanging off the back of the chair and on the floor. His rocking had slowed, at least. He was staring at his hands, which were spread out on the table.

Rebecca pressed record on the camera and entered the room. She stated the date and time for the recording.

"We found Clare."

There was a slight pause in his rocking.

"Mermaid." His voice was raw and shaky, but his eyes didn't shift. They stayed focused on his hands, staring at his crimson fingernails.

That was when she realized she'd broken her own rule. Not only was she without backup in the room, but there also wasn't anyone else in the building except for Viviane. He wasn't even cuffed.

Adrenaline flooded her system, prickling her nerves.

She leaned back in her chair to project a level of calm she did not feel and to subtly put more distance between them.

"Do you remember letting me check your phone? I looked at your messages with Clare."

He didn't respond.

She watched him for even the slightest reaction. Any sign that he was about to lose control.

"You two made plans to see each other last night."

"Mermaid." His lips barely moved as he spoke.

"Yeah, your sexy little mermaid. She's a nice *catch*." He flinched but didn't say anything. "I saw her, you know. She was laid out on her bed. Did you do that to her? Did you make her that tail from things you found on the beach?"

His gaze lifted from his hands to Rebecca's eyes.

She instinctively tensed. She braced for his next move and inched her hand toward her holster. His eyes tracked her motion and then returned to meet her gaze.

Silent tears trickled down his cheeks.

Is he acting? Is this remorse for his actions? Or grief for his loss? Does he plan to lawyer up?

"Malcolm, did you do that to Clare? Did you kill her? Did you kill your mermaid?"

His vacant eyes didn't react, except for the tears that poured from them. "Not mine…no. Not…"

Rebecca leaned to her right, but his eyes didn't follow her.

"Malcolm?"

Slowly his eyes shifted to the side, meeting hers again.

No. He was only looking at her mouth.

Leaning closer, she snapped her fingers a few inches in front of his face.

Malcolm's eyes slowly tracked to the left.

He wasn't seeing anything. Not her, not the phone. His attention was only focused on sounds.

Rebecca didn't think this was an act. Not unless this guy was a male Meryl Streep.

A loud knock echoed around the room.

Rebecca jumped, but the addled man just pivoted in his chair, trying to find the source of the noise.

She got up and walked sideways to the door, keeping Malcolm in sight. She opened the door and stepped out, pulling it closed and locking it.

Viviane was waiting on the other side of the hall. "How's he doing? Are you okay?"

Rebecca shook her head and swallowed hard. "Do you have any idea where the paramedics are?"

"No clue. They were called away a while ago and never returned. I don't expect they will either. Protocol says they stay until it's no longer safe and then they're required to evacuate." Viviane's eyes were wide. "Do you want me to try to call them back?"

Hell, she didn't know.

"He's not getting better or worse, so I'm honestly not sure what to do. I thought we'd be fine staying here, but now I wish I'd had him taken to the mainland." She growled low in her throat as she continued to second-guess herself.

Viviane squeezed her arm. "This is not a normal situation. Don't you go doubting yourself. Last time I looked, you didn't have a crystal ball."

Rebecca licked her lips. "But I'm a detective at heart. I should have seen this coming. What if he takes a turn for the worse? I have very little medical training and don't think I'd be much help to him."

"Darian can be back here in seven minutes if we need him. He called in to let me know. Said he was worried after you asked him about his *combats*?"

"Combatives. Yeah. Well, a lot can happen in seven minutes." Rebecca glanced through the viewing portal. The plexiglass was clean, and she had a good view of Malcolm as he stared blindly at the wall. "Whatever you do, do not open this door. Unless there's a fire. Even then, call me first."

"Yes, ma'am."

Her receptionist and friend looked a little scared. But in her heart, Rebecca knew that was a good thing. Fear would keep Viviane safe.

"Do you need me for something?"

"Oh, right!" Viviane palmed her forehead. "I'm sorry. Hoyt called in. He needs to talk to you. Said it's an emergency."

Rebecca groaned and leaned against the wall for a moment.

"Of course it is."

14

Rebecca followed Viviane out of the back hall and stepped into her office, where she'd left her radio when she went back to the interrogation room.

She lifted it to her mouth and clicked the mic. "West here. What's up? Over."

There was no response.

Viviane chewed her lower lip. "Uhm, even the handhelds are being a bit erratic due to the storm. Honestly, I'm surprised we haven't lost power here."

Rebecca sat on her desk and moved closer to the window for better reception. "West here for Hoyt. Over."

"Boss, I need help down here. Over."

The storm came through perfectly on the channel, but it was hard to make out Hoyt's voice against the lashing of the rain.

"Copy that. What kind of help and where? Over." She kept it brief and started using her other hand to put everything back on her belt or in her pockets.

"Walter Bolland...on his roof. He...stuck, and...can't get...adder..."

Adder?

It said a lot about her frame of mind that her first thought was that one of her deputies was calling for help while dealing with a snake.

"You need a ladder? Over." She raised her voice to be heard over the noise on his end.

"I have one. I need a second set of hands. No one else is responding. Over." This time he spoke slower, so each word came through without getting cut off.

"Address?"

"Viviane has it."

"Roger that. On my way. Over."

"What's wrong with people?" Viviane started gesturing with her hands. "I bet Mr. Bolland was trying to board up his windows, but the wind got too bad. His ladder started to fall, so he scrambled onto the roof."

"At least he didn't fall."

Viviane's dark eyes were wide. "Yeah, that would have been bad. Walter, Mr. Bolland, doesn't have grass. He's got rocks and driftwood and pampas grass. Nothing you would want to land on. Especially since, you know, the weather." She rambled as her hands jerked around.

She was scared.

Her dark skin was slightly pale. Sweat beaded on the side of her neck. Her eyes tightened at every crash of thunder.

Shit. She's been sitting here alone for how long now? With all this hanging over her head.

"Okay, Viviane, I need you to go back to your desk and send the address to my cruiser."

"On it, Boss."

She was trying so hard to be brave, but her eyes darted down the hall to the interrogation room.

"And once you're done with that, go ahead and forward the dispatch to my cell phone."

Viviane, who had been about to walk off, stopped. "Boss?"

Rebecca had no idea if she could handle everything, but she was going to try. "Send me the address to reach Hoyt, forward the calls to my number, then evacuate as soon as you can."

"Mama already took care of my packing and everything. Just in case. But…how can you do this on your own? You've got a prisoner back there."

Shit.

"See if we can get an ambulance back here. If we can, have the paramedics cuff him to a gurney and get him to a mainland hospital."

Viviane frowned. "I'll try, but the phones. How—?"

Rebecca waved her off. "I doubt phone service will be operational for much longer. I probably won't get any calls at all. Don't worry." She hoped Viviane believed her reassurances more than she did.

No need for her friend to worry. Rebecca was doing more than enough of that for the both of them. She did have a plan, but one that was just a notch below insane. Her stomach started to cramp from stress.

Why did she eat that chili?

Don't think about it.

"Viviane, please hurry. Hoyt's waiting for me. And your mom's waiting for you."

"But…" Viviane's eyes darted back and forth, and she started twisting her fingers. "Are you sure? I can't just leave you." She stepped forward and grabbed Rebecca's hand, clutching it in her cold one.

Rebecca squeezed her hand back.

"You can. And you will." She smiled at her friend. "That's an order."

"Yes, Boss." Viviane spun and ran to her desk. "I'll save you a margarita, so call me when you get out!"

"Will do." Rebecca gulped and was glad no one could see her. "Drive safely."

Pulling the keys from her belt, she walked out of her office and locked it behind her. Then, running because she knew Hoyt was waiting, Rebecca went through and locked every door, made sure every computer was powered down and picked up a cup of coffee and a cup of chili. The sloppy squish of her wet socks in her shoes echoed through the building, making everything seem so much eerier. She ran back through and yanked open the interrogation room door.

"Here's food and water."

Malcolm didn't look up as she set them down on the table in front of him. He was right back to studying his fingers.

She took the blanket from the floor and draped it over his shoulders again. For a moment, she struggled with deciding whether to tell him he could leave at any time or tell him to wait for her. But in the end, she figured not saying anything was best. Legally, she could not leave a suspect locked up alone in the building. But technically speaking, she hadn't arrested or even detained him, only confiscated some of his belongings. It was a gray legal matter.

A morally gray area too.

Rebecca hesitated. Leaving a man in the throes of what appeared to be a dissociative break alone during a hurricane was not the moral thing to do. But weighing all the available options, it was the lesser of all evils. Risking Viviane's safety was not a consideration. Leaving Hoyt alone to deal with his emergency was not a possibility. No one else had even responded to his pleas for assistance. She was out of options.

If Malcolm Jenner wasn't faking, he was safer here than outside. If he was faking, he could take this opportunity to make a run for it. But he had no vehicle, and the town was being evacuated. If he was guilty, he might take his chances and run. And they'd just have to track him down later and arrest him then. If he wasn't guilty, he would have no reason at all to run.

Dammit to hell.

Refusing to second-guess herself further, she made sure the interrogation door was unlocked before running for her coat and slamming through the front door. Using her keys one last time, she turned the outer lock but left the inner lock open. Malcolm Jenner was no longer being held in custody. He was a free man. If he decided to get up and walk out the door, there was nothing holding him back. She'd radio her deputies to let them know what she'd done.

Struggling against the wind, she ran to help her deputy save a man's life. She could only hope she wasn't putting other people's lives in danger by doing so.

15

Hoyt stood in Bolland's side yard. He'd hoped that, if he could drag the ladder to the side of the house out of the wind, he could use brute force to work it up the wall high enough for Walter to reach it.

But now he was fighting against the wind every time the top of the ladder got close to the roofline. Walter had followed him around to this side, and now was in a worse position than he had been before. This side of the roof had a decorative peak with a steep pitch.

The muscles in Hoyt's lower stomach screamed with every movement now. Every time the wind hit the ladder and shook it in his grasp, it felt like it was yanking on those muscles. It was an extension ladder, and he couldn't seem to hold it up while using the rope to extend it high enough to reach Walter's new perch.

The wet ladder was, once again, ripped from his grip and slammed to the ground. Hoyt collapsed to his knees next to it, twisted around by the whipping winds. His side cramped, and his thighs shook. He panted, trying to catch his breath now that he was no longer staring face-first into the rain.

His throat burned as he coughed up some rain that had poured into him.

Stay down. Rest until West gets here.

A cry from behind him made him lift his head. The wind blew directly in his face, forcing his eyes open wide, and he had to consciously work against it to pull air into his lungs.

Walter was clinging to the side of his roof. His fingers dug into the rough asphalt shingles as he desperately tried not to be swept down the steep pitch by the sheets of water funneling past him. His face was twisted. Hoyt could see that he was screaming, even though he couldn't hear him.

Shit!

Hoyt pounded his fist on the ground, splashing sandy water back up into his face. He couldn't wait for his boss.

He had to use both hands to lever his body up again as his knees wobbled. Bracing his hands on his knees helped him to stand, but it hurt his back and side even more. With a loud grunt, he forced himself mostly upright and turned back to the house. He had to try again. There wasn't a minute to lose.

At least there was no lightning, so he didn't have to worry about getting electrocuted. Focusing on moving one foot in front of the other, he grabbed the ladder for another try.

Blue-and-red lights reflected off the wet siding of the house. Backup had arrived.

Oh, thank you, God!

West slid her cruiser into the curb from braking too late and hydroplaning the last few feet. Lifting his arms despite the pain, he waved to flag her down, then realized she likely couldn't see him. He stepped into the glow of her headlights.

As soon as the Explorer finished bouncing, West jumped out and ran over.

"Where?" she screamed as she raced up.

"There!" He pointed to where Walter was sliding closer to

the drop. The man's feet were braced against the gutter now. Its thin aluminum wouldn't hold for long.

West grabbed the ladder in the middle and unlocked the catches to draw the extension back down. It was half completed by the time Hoyt made it to her side.

She took one look at his hunched stance, and he knew she knew. Her head jerked up to where Walter hung, then followed a line down to the ground nearly fifteen feet away from the foundation of the house. With a shake of her head, she started dragging the ladder to the spot she had picked out. He stooped to help her, but she motioned him back and flipped the ladder around, setting the feet down.

"I can't keep it up there in this wind. It keeps blowing over." He yelled next to her head as he stepped up to help her get the feet planted.

"You anchor it!" She pointed at the bottom rung. "I'll raise the extension."

Well, at least I'm good for something.

West stood at least four inches shorter than him, and she had to be more than fifty pounds lighter. And it was going to take every pound to keep this ladder stable once they got it up again. This wasn't her being nice to him because of his injury. This was the only way this had a chance of working.

He passed the rope for the extension to her and hopped onto the rung, driving the feet into the loose, decorative gravel and sand surrounding the house.

All the jugs, driftwood, and water features that usually filled out the stone garden were gone. The fool man had taken those in the house first and put off the more challenging work of boarding up the windows 'til last. Like so many others on the island, he probably thought this hurricane was going to turn again before it reached them and boarding the windows was overkill. Until the sirens had sounded, and the radio announcements forced him to face reality.

It took both of them to hold the bottom of the ladder in place while still keeping the rest of it upright enough to extend. West used one hand to brace. With the other, she pulled the ladder up. Doing it that way only lifted it two rungs at a time. But the wind slipping around the side of the house demanded three hands to keep it from tipping over.

West cursed the entire time, wishing loudly that she'd thought to bring some thick gloves. The rope burning the hell out of her palms brought out further complex expletives.

Hoyt was a little impressed at how creative and long-winded her tirade was.

It was almost enough for him to ignore the growing pain in his weakened muscles. Still, he kept looking up to see how close they were to reaching Walter. The ladder extended less than a foot at a time now, fighting against the wind and gravity. But they were close.

Walter was dealing with the same problem. He kept looking over his shoulder, monitoring how close it was coming.

"Stop turning, you idiot! You're going to fall!"

No sooner had the words left Hoyt's mouth than Walter's grip gave. Or maybe it was the shingle that tore loose.

"Use both hands!" Hoyt screamed at West, hoping she heard him.

"What?"

"Use! Both! Hands! He's falling!" Hoyt braced himself. Flipping his grip, he braced his elbows on the rungs and straddled the ladder. He squatted, pulling and holding with all his might.

Three pulls. That was all. He just had to hold on for three more pulls of the rope.

I can do it. I can do it. I can do it.

The clangs of the catches slapping at a rapid pace vibrated through his body, shaking his exhausted muscles. It felt like he'd been tased. The muscles he'd pulled that morning were cramping so hard he thought they would snap. Even worse, there was an odd numb spot just over his left hip.

"Lift!" The ladder jerked. "Hoyt! Lift! We're almost there!"

Hoyt opened his eyes.

The top of the ladder was just below the roof's overhang and right below Walter's dangling foot.

West was pushing back against the ladder. He leaned with her as she pulled one last time. The ladder slammed down on the roofline, shuddering as the wind beat at it.

"Walter! To your left!" West screamed against the rain, ending with a cough.

But the man on the roof could not hear them.

"Shit!" West screamed and yanked the ladder to the side. The edge slapped into Walter's dangling foot.

He recoiled in fear, then seemed to realize what had happened and looked down. Now all he had to do was let go and slide down far enough to reach the ladder. As long as he didn't fall. He stretched out his lower leg and managed to wiggle his foot onto the top rung.

Slowly, he worked his lower body to that side until both feet were on the ladder. Hoyt got a good look at the man's shoes. He was wearing slippers. *Slippers.*

The ladder shook with the added weight at its highest point. West twisted, clutching onto the rungs from the bottom side at their widest point to hold it in place. They were nearly face to face through the spaces on the ladder.

West had her eyes squeezed shut as if she were in pain. It fell on Hoyt to watch Walter climb down and make sure he didn't misstep.

Not that he could do a damn thing if that happened.

An eternity later, Hoyt had to step back out of Walter's way as he finally placed his feet on the ground.

"Thank you. Oh, thank you. I thought I was going to die alone. Then I thought I was going to die right in front of you. Then, when you collapsed, I thought we were going to die together." Walter babbled on, twisting back and forth as he stared at each of them. "You really are a hero. Just like the papers said. You, too, Hoyt, of course. You're a hero too."

If it wouldn't have caused him so much pain, Hoyt would have laughed at that. Instead, he nodded as he massaged his aching guts.

"Good to hear. So to keep our winning streak going and make sure no one dies here today, how about you go ahead and hop in your car and leave. Has your wife left already?"

"Yeah. She headed out this morning with the kids. I told her I'd take care of everything here and then meet up with her." He was nodding nonstop. "I was putting away the lawn furniture when the sirens went off. I still need to board up the last windows." His gaze lifted to the precarious perch he had just been freed from.

"Too bad about that. But you need to leave now."

"Could you give me a hand with the last ones? My wife is going to be so mad at me if I don't get them all and something happens."

West stepped around from the ladder, massaging her right shoulder. "You really think we're going to hold the ladder down while you climb up it with a sheet of plywood? Are you trying to kill yourself or us? Death by plywood is not the way I want to go!"

He looked surprised but finally nodded as she held a fierce glare on him.

The myrtle tree next to the street took that opportunity to bend and split in half as the wind picked up speed even more.

"Yeah. No. I don't want to kill anyone. Or die. I'm going now. Just need to lock up the house."

"We'll lock the house. Do you have your keys?" Making sure not to use his ab muscles, Hoyt turned the man toward his driveway and the car waiting there.

"Yeah." He pulled them from his pocket and held them up.

"Good. Now go meet your wife. She'll kill you if you end up dead."

"Yeah." Walter nodded several more times but moved on his own power as he climbed into his car and backed out of the driveway, plowing through the standing water.

As they watched the man drive away in his sopping wet slippers, a loud clatter caused Hoyt to twist and duck, tweaking his aching muscles even more.

Walter's ladder narrowly missed them both.

16

"Are you okay?" Hoyt asked as West stared at the ladder inches from their feet.

"What?" she yelled back.

Hoyt sighed and pointed at the front door. She nodded.

Ducking his head against the wind, Hoyt and West fought to remain upright as the horizontal rain lashed at them. Like mimes walking in place, they barely made progress to the front door. Just as Walter had said, it was unlocked, and Hoyt stepped inside the relative quiet.

West followed and gave a relieved sigh.

"I was asking if you were okay." Hoyt started walking through the house, turning off the lights.

"I'm fine. I didn't even hear the ladder crash to the ground. The real question is, are *you* okay?"

"I'm better now that we're out of the rain."

She rotated her shoulder and groaned.

He tried not to stare as she worked through her own pain.

She caught him, though, and gave a self-conscious laugh. "My shoulder is shot. Well, it was shot. Took a bullet back in D.C. Acts up when I overdo it."

Hoyt nodded, piecing things together in his mind. "That part of the...*drama* that sent you down our way?"

"Drama." West snorted. "Yeah, the drama. Got ambushed waiting for a drop-off that would pinpoint the moneyman behind my parents' murder. It was in a parking garage."

A bunch of other pieces fell into place for him. "Well, that explains the smell thing." He shrugged and turned to finish his task. "And since we're sharing, my gut is all messed up after today. Pulled something I shouldn't have."

Concern clouded her expression. "Do you need to clock out?"

Hoyt scoffed. "I will when you do."

West smiled. "Noted. However, you do get to stand still for a while. Before you get back to the evacuation route, you should stop by the station. Angie's already left, but she and some others left a stockpile of food there."

Hearing his wife's name brought up a rush of protective instincts, and Hoyt sucked in a full breath as he thought of Angie in the fierce winds he'd just escaped.

"Did I hear you radio that you'd left our suspect's door unlocked?"

She blew out a deep breath. "Yeah. With this weather, it felt like the right thing to do. To be honest, I have no idea if it was a good idea or stupid as hell."

He didn't know, either, but he understood why she did it.

"We'll worry about him later. One problem at a time."

West reached into her pocket and pulled out her phone. She stared at the screen in disbelief. "How are these things even still working? It's like the apocalypse out there, and I'm still getting calls. I think my provider should turn this into their next commercial."

While she took the call, Hoyt tried his wife.

Angie answered immediately. "Breaker breaker, Big Daddy, did you miss me already?"

Hoyt laughed so hard he winced with pain. "Every minute of every day." As always, hearing her voice was like a balm to his emotions.

Angie giggled, and his heart skipped a beat. "Oh, you charmer you. Really, though, what's wrong? Why are you calling?"

"Just wanted to make sure you got out okay."

"Well, I got in the car okay. But right now, I'm stuck in traffic. We're not stopped, it's just slow." Her voice softened. "Can you leave soon?"

He didn't want to lie to her, but he didn't want to worry her either. "Yeah. As soon as I can."

"Well, I've got your bags, and the house is all boarded up. I secured the storm shutters and moved everything inside. You don't need to do a thing except get off the island."

"You're amazing. What did I ever do that was good enough to deserve you?"

"Oh, you know what you did."

The loving tone in his wife's voice sent Hoyt's heart racing. He knew exactly what she was talking about.

His own voice dropped a few octaves in response. "I do. And I'll do it again."

West coughed loudly, and he remembered he didn't actually have any privacy here.

"Duty calls, dear. I love you. Drive safe. And contact me when you get to your mom's."

"Love you too. And I'll hold you to your promise. Over and out, stud."

Oh, he knew she'd hold him to it. He knew he was grinning like a fool when he turned back to face his boss, but he didn't care.

"I take it your wife is fine."

Hoyt's grin grew. "She's mighty fine, yes, ma'am."

West chuckled, then grabbed her shoulder. "I'll make you

a deal. Neither one of us makes the other one laugh for the rest of the day."

He ran his hand over his strained muscles. "Deal. Does the bad shoulder hurt as bad as the bad abs?"

"No clue. But I'm betting they both suck in their own ways."

That was a fair point, so he nodded. "Who called you? Could it be that you have a special someone who's evacuating too?" He thought his teasing would at least get a blush. Ryker should be leaving the island about now.

Sadly, his taunt went unnoticed as her phone rang again.

"Sheriff's office, this is Sheriff West, what's your emergency?" West's smile melted away as she listened to the caller. "I understand. Officers are on their way. Stay in your cars and continue evacuating the island."

Hoyt's heart sank. "What was that about?"

Please don't let it be another idiot on a roof.

"Yeah. About that. I ordered Viviane to evacuate. I've got dispatch transferring to my phone for now. I'd hoped folks would lose cell service, and it wouldn't ring. But that call was from 911. The winds are causing debris to crash into the bridge pillars. And the levees are failing. Coastal Drive is being flooded by the waves."

His heart threatened to punch through his chest.

Coastal Drive was the evacuation route Viviane and Angie were on.

And there was not a damn thing he could do about it.

17

It was a fight, but Rebecca convinced Hoyt to go to Darian's position and swap places. She planned to go back to the sandbags and help shore up the line, so they could hopefully get more vehicles off the island. Hoyt volunteered to help, but after struggling with the ladder on his own for so long, he would be slower than someone who had been standing around for the last few hours.

They both left Walter's house with lights flashing. Rebecca got two more phone calls in that short drive and argued with the callers that the evacuation was real. No, it was not a siren test in the middle of the storm.

Having learned from her last stop, she slowed down well before reaching the sandlot, cursing as her abraded palms moved over the steering wheel. The adrenaline rush from earlier had worn off, as did the analgesic effect that went with it. Now her hands burned like hell.

There were already a few people gathered around two trucks. Flipping on her spotlight, she pointed it toward the gathering.

She couldn't hear them over the pounding of the rain on

her roof, but their fists pumping over their heads indicated they were cheering her arrival.

Grabbing her earpiece, she popped it in and climbed out of the car to join them. Even with the added light, she had to get closer before recognizing Ryker's truck.

"Glad to have you back!" He smiled down at her as he caught the next bag while bracing against the fierce winds.

"Feels like I never left." Despite the terrible weather and circumstances, she couldn't help but grin. "What's the plan?"

"We're trying to divert water off Coastal Drive, so fill up any bags we can find and get them out there as fast as possible."

"I'll join the line for a bit. I'm no good with a shovel."

Three people were standing under the nominal cover of an awning and feverishly working to fill bags. Some were burlap. Others looked like woven plastic. Some were clearly brought in from the produce section of grocery stores.

Rebecca moved along the line until people shifted to make a gap for her. The bags got heavier the farther they went as the already damp sand soaked up the rain.

The downpour pattered and pinged around them while she turned to the left, took a bag, turned to the right, and passed it on, wincing each time her hands made contact.

There was no talking, except for the phone call she answered by pressing her earbud against her shoulder. That got her a few looks, and someone laughed. But she just shrugged and explained that, yes, there was flooding in the town, and they needed to evacuate.

"You shoulda told 'em to come down here and help," the man she passed the bag to yelled.

"If they're that oblivious, do you really want them building a wall?"

He bobbed his head as he laughed, then he paused.

Rebecca had already turned to take the next bag. When

she turned back to hand him another, she saw he was still holding the last.

Frowning and bent over, he twisted the bag in the light. "Why is there blood on this bag?"

She could barely hear him. "What?"

He held the bag up so she could see it. "The bag's bloody!"

Rebecca looked down at the one in her hands. "This one isn't." She shifted it around to show him and exposed a bloody mark. "What the hell?"

She twisted to her left, and the man moved with her as they checked the bag waiting to be passed to her.

"This next one's clean." She shrugged, confused about what was happening.

The man took the bag from her and passed it on before leading her over to a work light. As she started to protest, he grabbed her hand and flipped it over.

"Oh." The blisters on her palms had broken open. Now that she could see the burns, cuts, and rope splinters, they started to sting, and she was grateful for the rain pouring into them.

"The hell! How long have you been out here working?" The man to her left flipped over her other hand and inspected it. That one was just as severely burned.

Rebecca blinked at him as she tried to remember.

Both men stared.

"They're fine. It barely hurts."

"This sand is filthy! You need to wear some gloves, at least."

She started to reach for the pouch on her back, then stopped and shook her head. "I don't have any that will work. I…" Suddenly remembering the ones she'd put in the evidence kit, she turned to retrieve them. "I'll go get some."

Hurrying from the line, she didn't hear what they yelled after her but just waved her hand. It was easier to walk here than anywhere else in town. Spilled sand was layered thick in the gravel of the lot and provided plenty of traction. Inside the back of the SUV, she pulled open the kit and started digging around.

Lights came up behind her, and she turned to see Darian pull up in his cruiser. She waved him up next to her and finally found the work gloves. She tried to pull on the latex gloves first, not wanting to get more sand or dirty leather into the cuts. The tight-fitting material snagged on the jagged strands of nylon rope that stuck out of her palms.

She hissed in pain and held them up to the light of the liftgate to see how long the strands were. Of course, they were long enough to snag the latex but not long enough for her to get a grip on and pull out.

"Taking a break, Boss? Did you bring a carafe by any chance?" Darian leaned over her shoulder to peer into the back of the vehicle and saw what she was doing. "Something wrong?"

Rebecca sighed, feeling stupid for no good reason as she watched the blood dripping from her hand. "I got rope burn hauling a ladder up, and now I can't get my gloves over these splinters."

Darian arched an eyebrow, asking for permission.

When she nodded, he took her fingertips and stretched her hand open. "Damn. I'm not even going to ask what you were doing with Ryker to end up like this."

"Ha ha. You're talking about *wood,* right?"

He laughed, his light brown eyes lighting up. "You said it, not me."

"Well, for your information, this is from a rope, not wood, so your gutter mind can calm down." She rolled her eyes and ignored the ribbing about her possible love life. "If I had some duct tape, I could pull them out."

He grinned, then flicked open a pocketknife and held it up. "I've got the next best thing."

It was only about three inches long and had a slight curve. The light glinted on the blade, and she was sure it was razor sharp. She'd never known an Army soldier who let a knife go dull.

Rebecca stared at him, then took a deep breath. "Do it."

He froze. "I was just joking."

"Half joke, all truth. I can't work like this. The splinters will get shoved in even deeper. I've already driven with them and handled who knows how many sandbags. Scrape them out. Or give me the knife, and I'll try." Her hands were already starting to stiffen with pain and swelling, so she had no idea if she could manage it herself.

"You're serious?"

"Hudson." She glared at him.

"You're sure?"

"Darian! Do it before they start to regain feeling, dammit!"

He adjusted his grip and moved her hand into a better position. "I'm just asking because my wife insists that only we grunts are dumb enough to do something like this." He laid the blade down on her palm, angled like he was about to stroke it on a whetstone.

"They do it for fun. We do it when we've got work to do. Now, get to it."

He chuckled his agreement and bent over her hand again. "Yes, sir."

Darian pulled the blade slowly and forcefully down her palm from her fingers in the opposite direction of the splinters to force them out.

"But don't think less of me when I start cursing." She spoke through clenched teeth.

"Never."

The blade bumped over the first cut in her palm, dragging the torn flesh open and ripping out the large nylon pieces that had left her hands resembling a porcupine.

"Shiiiiiiiiiiiiiiiiiiiit." Rebecca gasped but did her best not to jerk her hand. How in the hell had she managed not to notice that while driving over here?

Darian's grip tightened on her wrist as the blade got close to it.

"Don't twitch."

"You either." She grunted, then clenched her jaw. Her hand felt like she'd grabbed a hot poker. After what seemed like hours, Darian released her wrist, and she jerked it away to shake, releasing the tension that had built up.

She knew Darian was testing her mettle as a leader, and she wasn't going to back down. Not because she cared about a dick-measuring contest, but because she really did want to return to work.

"Ready for the other one?"

She thrust her hand out. "You sure you don't want to refresh the lemon juice you keep your knife soaked in?"

"Oh, don't be silly, Sheriff. It's not soaked in lemon juice." He adjusted her hand and pressed the blade against it after wiping it off on his trousers. "It's soaked in saltwater."

He started dragging the blade down again, and she snorted. "Fuuuu-uuu-oh, dammit. Don't make me laugh. Oh shit."

"Stop laughing! You made me miss." He moved the blade back up to go over the same spot.

Rebecca bit her lips, making sure not to move so he wouldn't have to restart again. He finished scraping her other hand and wiped his blade off once more.

She turned her palms up and inspected them. They burned like blazes, but there was noticeably less resistance when she flexed them.

"You got a first aid kit?" Darian peered at his handiwork.

"I do. But nothing that's going to work in this weather. That's why I was going to put the gloves on."

"Put them on inside out. You don't want to get that powder in those cuts. It will dry them out and make 'em worse."

"Good thinking." Rebecca wanted desperately to press her burning flesh against the cool metal of the car but knew that was a bad plan. The rain had a sting to it that was at least partially salt spray. And she knew Darian hadn't been joking when he said his knife was soaked in seawater. With the hurricane moving in, everything was covered in saltwater.

Instead, she struggled to get her gloves flipped inside out and over her aching hands.

"Go ahead and go help load up the trucks. I'll join you shortly."

"Yes, sir. And if anyone asks, I never heard you curse." He tapped his brim with the side of his fingers and steeled himself against the rainy onslaught, letting her calm down after her painful experience.

As soon as he was gone, she rested her head against the side of her cruiser, letting the cool metal soothe her as she took several slow, deep breaths. Darian had missed the splinters in her thumbs, but she hadn't had the guts to tell him. Everything else had been too much to deal with.

The entire day had been too much to deal with.

How long have I been working out here?

She checked her watch. Ten fifteen.

Unless something had changed, Boris would be here in less than six hours.

She didn't have time to rest or complain. Once she got this done and the levees rebuilt, she could go back to the office and make sure Malcolm Jenner was still alive and hadn't wandered off. Maybe she could even sit down with a cup of coffee for a minute.

Rebecca's earbud chirped as yet another call came in.

Thankfully, there was no one close enough to hear her, and she let loose a string of curses that would've made a sailor blush.

18

Rebecca took a deep breath. "Shadow Island Sheriff's Department, Sheriff West speaking, what's your emergency?"

"Sheriff West, this is Richmond Vale."

Her teeth ground together in frustration. What could the asshole possibly want now?

Rebecca was glad the chairman had been on vacation because she couldn't imagine dealing with her previous cases with him around the island.

"Hello, Mr. Vale. How can I help you?"

"I just wanted to let you know that there's a storm shelter inside the town hall. With you being new and all, I wasn't sure if you knew about it. For anyone who can't get off the island in time or find a safe place, they can come here. We've got first aid, food, water, and even some cots."

"Oh...okay." Rebecca tried to wrap her head around the idea of Vale being worried about someone else. From everything she'd heard about him, he only cared about himself. Then he really blew her mind.

"That includes you and all your men. I know you're out

working the streets, making sure everyone is safe. But once it gets too dangerous, I want you all to know there's a safe place waiting for you."

"Sir, I greatly appreciate that. I'll be certain to remind my men. Right now, we're out here bagging more sand to rebuild some of the levees that weren't high enough to hold back the floodwaters."

There was another pause, and Rebecca heard mumbling in the background.

"Mayor Doughtie wants to know if you need more bodies out there."

Now it all made sense. Doughtie was pushing Vale to do this. That was why he sounded so wooden. It was the mayor's words coming out of his mouth.

"We'll take all the hands we can get." She remembered the produce bags she'd seen in the stack to be used. "And if you know where there are any more sandbags to fill, that would be extremely helpful. We're using anything we can get our hands on now."

"I gave all the bags we could find to one of the crew leaders. The mayor's already brought him everything he could from town as well. I'm afraid everything we have is already at the sandlot."

"Then that will have to be enough. I'm here with Ryker now, filling them up."

"Good, and just in case you all haven't heard, landfall is estimated a little earlier than expected. Around three thirty now."

A chill ran up Rebecca's spine. "Then I need to get back to sandbagging. We've got to keep Coastal Drive passable."

"Good luck, Sheriff."

Rebecca ended the uncomfortable call and slammed the liftgate closed. Running as fast as she could against the onslaught of wind and rain, she headed back to the truck.

She shoved her gloves on over the latex pair, wincing in pain as the leather squeezed her swollen digits.

"Ryker!"

His head didn't even raise as he stacked bags methodically.

"Ryker!" He still didn't hear her, so she leaped up, grabbed the side of the bed, and swung herself in next to him.

He jerked back as she landed with one foot on the bags and stumbled. "What's up?"

"ETA is now three thirty. How bad does that screw us up?" She stared at him wide-eyed, forgetting everything else for the moment.

Darian, standing on the line close to the truck, had moved closer when she arrived. "We can clear out the people that are in line to get out now if we can stop the washouts. But not many more. The storm surge is already above high tide. It won't be long before the sea swells will get too bad."

He and Ryker shared a look.

"Then we need to get there ASAP if we're going to get off this island too." Ryker raised his voice. "Okay, folks, we need to speed this up."

A few of the heads closest to them nodded, but the rest didn't react. Most of the workers barely managed to stand against the driving elements. The rain was coming in sideways.

"Ay!" Darian's voice boomed louder than the thunder, and everyone jerked to stare at him. "Double time! Go! Go! Go!"

"Damn, Darian, I didn't know you were a drill sergeant." Rebecca laughed as she struggled down from the truck bed and tossed filled bags up beside Ryker. The work was made easy because the wind was coming from behind her, practically lifting the bags for her. Ryker, however, was getting slammed by the projectiles.

"No, sir. I worked for my living." Darian grinned and

started chucking the bags overhand into Ryker's truck. Ryker stopped trying to catch the missiles and, instead, positioned them after they landed.

"I'll bring my truck around to start filling up too." A woman pushed against the wind, clutching her keys as she passed.

"Good idea. We don't need the trucks full before they take off. And once everyone has dropped off their bags, they need to get off the island." Rebecca nodded to Darian, who turned his body to act as her megaphone.

"Last load up! Gonna fill, drop, then evacuate the island. Two-hour limit!"

The woman with the truck pulled up closer to the sandbaggers. Ryker took that as his cue. "I'm heading out. See you all on the other side."

Rebecca reached out and grabbed his arm, unable to stop herself. "Stay safe."

Ryker turned with a heart-stopping smile that made her legs wobble. "You too."

He grabbed her hand, and she widened her eyes so she wouldn't wince at the burning pain. She managed to squeeze his hand in return, then worked her way over to where the line was reforming.

Darian took the place of two people, grabbing a bag in each hand and tossing them into the truck.

"Don't worry about stacking them!" the woman yelled, running to pick up a shovel. "Just get them in as fast as possible."

Rebecca positioned herself next to Darian, catching one bag at a time and handing them to him on one side while another man took up the other side.

"I don't know, but I been told…" Darian turned to smile at her. His grin looked slightly nuts in the flashing rain. "That my boss is getting old."

Hiding her laugh with a glare, Rebecca responded in kind. "I don't know, but I've been told, Hurricane Boris is mighty bold." His grin got even wider as she sang the next line. "But in his path is a group of friends, who stack bags high for their isle's defense. Sound off!"

Darian burst out laughing. "One, two." He chucked two bags.

A woman's voice picked up the cadence behind them. "I don't know, but it's been said, Boris's arms are made of lead. I don't know, but I've been told, islanders' wings are made of gold. Sound off!"

"One two!" Several voices rose with the well-known line.

"Sound off!" Darian called again.

"Three four!"

"One, two, one, two, three, four!"

A scattered chorus of oorah, hooah, and hooyah, rang out from the gathering, representing every military branch.

As always, singing sped up the work and lightened the moods of everyone gathered as well. The truck bed was half loaded now. Most of the bags were piled up in the middle, but that was fine. None of them were over the lip of the bed, and the weight was centered well enough.

"That's it!" the guy next to Rebecca shouted.

She turned, taking the bag from him, and saw that there were no more coming up the line. They were out.

Darian called out to the driver of the truck as he tossed the last two bags in. Rebecca heaved hers as well.

"Yo!" The truck owner came running up, pitching her shovel into the bed as well.

"Follow me out. I'll give you an escort."

"We'll follow you too." The men behind Rebecca scattered to their vehicles. "And get them unloaded."

"Darian!" Rebecca waited 'til he turned to look at her. "Do you know where you're going?"

His jaw fell open. "Uhh."

"Thought so. Follow me, everyone. Darian, you bring up the rear."

"Yes, sir!" Chagrined, he turned and jogged back to his vehicle.

Rebecca wondered what went through Darian's head that he couldn't decide if he should refer to her as ma'am or sir. She'd told that wet-behind-the-ears FBI agent to call her ma'am or sir or Sheriff because she didn't care. But since overhearing her say so, Darian had taken to switching back and forth. He'd even dropped the sardonic tone he'd started with, saying it with respect either way, so she wasn't perturbed.

Hopping in her cruiser, she left her gloves on. There was no telling if she would get them on again later. Even though they ached, the binding would keep the swelling down as much as possible.

Hitting her lights, Rebecca pulled to the end of the lot and waited as the other vehicles lined up behind her. Once more than half of them were in tow, she led the way through town and toward the bridge.

Rebecca drove on the left side of the road to get around slower-moving traffic. The break was at the turn just before the bridge, the worst possible place to have it fail. It was easy to find once they got close, as the water on the road got deeper. Throwing her cruiser into park and setting the emergency brake, Rebecca left it running and shoved against the wind to open her door.

She stopped traffic and waved the truck with bags into the line of cars. The person she stopped leaned forward, staring at her as she held her hand up in front of him, then swiveled as the truck pulled in.

In a move that no longer surprised her, the driver parked his car and jumped out into the deluge to join them. More islanders from the cars sitting in line spilled out of their vehicles and ran up to wade through the water next to the truck.

Several flashlights turned on in several cars, their beams running over the edge of the road until they all found, and focused on, where the water was spilling over the four-layer-high wall. There was nothing for Rebecca to do as citizens piled into the truck bed and lined up on the ground, bracing against the torrent, passing sandbags down and stacking them on the wall.

The overflow slowed, shifted, then stopped. Still, the sandbags were piled on, barricading against what they now knew would be a continuously rising tide and storm surge.

Cheers went up as the last bag was laid, and everyone made their way back to their cars.

Rebecca called out her thanks and got a few waves in return. The line ahead had thinned out as more cars made it over the bridge. Without struggle, the caravan was integrated into the single-file line. People could, once again, safely navigate the low spot in the roadway without worrying about their engines getting flooded.

With a sigh of relief at another catastrophe averted, Rebecca returned to the shelter of her cruiser. In her rearview mirror, she could see the other cruiser making a three-point turn, and she knew Darian was heading back to his assigned position.

Now she could return to the station and see if Malcolm Jenner was still there or if he had taken the opportunity to flee.

As much as she hated to admit it, she was almost too tired to care which scenario awaited her.

19

When Rebecca pulled up in front of the sheriff's station, the lights were still on. She peered in through the window but saw nothing out of the ordinary. There were no lurking shadows, no glowing computer screens that should have been off, nothing showing that anyone had moved within the building after she left.

She unlocked the door and shed her raincoat, freeing her arms to provide easier access to her sidearm. Getting the glove off her right hand was trickier, and she had to use her teeth to do so. The thick leather wouldn't fit in the trigger guard, and there was no way she would take that risk.

Rebecca walked through the lobby as quietly as possible, hands free of the gloves, her eyes constantly roving. Having to clear the station, which should have been the most secure location for her, frayed her nerves. The slow cookers were warm, and the scent of delicious meals filled the cool air.

So far, there was nothing to find. Every door she passed, she checked to make sure it was still locked. All of them were. The door of the interrogation room came into view as she turned the last corner. Stepping wide, she approached the viewing pane.

Malcolm Jenner sat in his chair, staring at his hands. The blanket she'd tucked around him had slipped down a little but was still snug between his back and the chair. Something was different about him, so she stayed in the hall until she could figure it out.

He's not rocking! Is he finally starting to come out of it?

Rebecca opened the door. "Mr. Jenner, can I get you anything?"

Malcolm's body tensed. He'd heard her. That was the first time he'd shown such a reaction since he'd arrived. His fingers scratched at the blanket on his upper arm.

"Mermaid."

"Yes, Mr. Jenner. We found the mermaid. We have her." Rebecca stepped forward, trying not to make any distracting moves or sounds. "Can you tell me about your mermaid?"

His head bobbed. "Mermaid."

She glanced at the cups she'd left on the table. They hadn't been touched. She moved into the room while trying not to intrude on him. "What about the mermaid?"

The bobbing of his head continued, along with his chant. "Mermaid."

Nothing else she said seemed to get through to him. She wasn't even confident he was responding to her questions with his constant response, "Mermaid." To test that theory, she sat there in silence.

"Mermaid."

The steady drum of rain was so fast and heavy that it sounded softer somehow, like waves crashing instead of a machine gun firing. Maybe it was because the wind was hitting the building more from the side than on the roof.

"Mermaid."

Rebecca sighed. He hadn't been answering her, only mumbling to himself.

"I understand, Mr. Jenner. I'll be right outside when you're ready to talk about what happened."

As she walked past him, she pulled the blanket up to his shoulders again. His skin wasn't clammy any longer, but still should be warmer. It was clear to her now that Malcolm Jenner wasn't faking his breakdown. And she had, so far, been right to leave him where he was and give him time to recover, just as Sandra Baker had said.

The next stop for her was the coffeepot. She poured a cup of dark sludge and grimaced. *How long has this been here?* She looked up at the clock on the wall.

Nearly eleven thirty. *Crap, no wonder I'm so exhausted.*

"Nothing like eight-hour-old coffee to keep you going, though." Rebecca busied herself making a fresh pot, and then unlocked her office door. She gathered up three cups. One of biscuits and gravy, one of a hearty-smelling broth, and the third was her burnt coffee to keep her company while she awaited the fresh pot. She'd already learned her lesson of mixing chili and stress and did not want a repeat of that.

Cradling the cups in her arm, she made her way back to her office and the first aid kit stored there. She set everything down before examining her hands. They had looked bad before she'd had them scraped out. Now they looked worse.

Her palms were pink and inflamed. Faded yellow, broken strands of brittle nylon remained. She recalled the burning, scratching pain as she yanked on the rope as it bit into her hands, but she hadn't thought she'd done this much damage with such a small rope.

Then again, her hands had been numb at the time, thanks to a combination of fear and adrenaline.

"This is going to suck when the feeling returns." She got

up and headed for the bathroom with a sigh and a bracing chug of coffee. Slathering her hands in soap, she started to scrub the shallow wounds but had to stop as the stinging pain exploded.

"Oh yeah. Chili would have been a bad idea."

She had to take a shaky breath before she could continue. Hot water and antibacterial soap hurt more than the knife treatment Darian had given her. There was no taking her time with this as the pain started clawing up her wrists and arms, the nerves in her hands protesting their abuse.

Once the last of the suds were rinsed down the drain, she turned off the hot water and sighed with relief as cold water took over. Her hands still hurt, but the pain was less and continued to recede the longer she bathed them.

She shook her chilled hands and grabbed several paper towels to take back to her desk. Numb would be best before she started digging around in them to pull out the rest of the splinters. Dropping down in her office chair, she said a silent *thank you* for the one thing providing her comfort today.

"That you, Boss?" Hoyt's voice echoed through the bullpen.

"Yup, it's me. How's the evacuation going?"

His footsteps squelched as he walked to her office. She pulled out the tweezers from the kit and started picking at her hands. Her fingers were thick, and her hands didn't want to move. While she could get a grip on the nylon, she couldn't pull hard enough to rip any of them free.

The squelches stopped at her door, and she looked up. Hoyt was leaning on the doorframe, frowning at her. "I was going to ask if you were raised in a barn, leaving your coat and gloves in the entryway like that. But I think I can see why you did."

"Sorry about that. I needed my hands free. I'd left Jenner

alone here, not locked up, and didn't want to take any chances."

"Eh, at least you made fresh coffee. Thanks for that." He motioned with his cup to her hands. "You do that hauling up the ladder?"

She frowned, wondering how he could tell from so far away.

"I heard you cursing and screaming. It looked like you were in pain. I thought it was your shoulder after we got in. Didn't realize you'd messed up your hands."

Rebecca's cheeks heated up at the realization that he'd heard her.

"Need some help with that? I've got a pocketknife." His eyes twinkled with the same mischief Darian's had.

She shook her head and continued to pick, trying to find one loose enough to slide out. "Already did that. I got out the big pieces, but I'm having the devil's own luck getting out the small bits." Giving up, she switched to her thumb pads, where there were still some longer ones.

He moved into the room to get a better look. "They both that bad?"

"Yup." Just thinking about them made the pain worse, and her hand started to twitch. "Dammit. I cannot do this."

"Want me to give it a shot?"

No!

"Please." Rebecca laid her hand out on the desk and picked up her coffee. "Jenner didn't leave, by the way." She started talking to distract herself as Hoyt sank into a guest chair.

He turned her hand around, trying to see the pieces in the light, and picked up the tweezers she'd relinquished.

"He didn't even move as far as I could tell." She sipped her coffee, and her gaze traveled around the room, looking at anything except her hand as the tugs started. "Didn't eat or drink anything either. But he does feel warmer to the touch. And he's talking. Just the same word over and over, though. He just keeps saying *mermaid* in a broken monotone voice."

Hoyt grunted. "So he's coming out of it. That's good. Hard to take a man to trial when he doesn't even know his name or where he is. But did you really think leaving him alone was a good idea?"

"No, I thought it was a terrible idea. But what else was I supposed to do? Let Walter die? Like you said, no one else heard your calls for assistance." She bit her lip and stared at the ceiling as a long pull traveled through her thumb. Hoyt had managed to get another one loose, and it felt like it started at her thumbnail and ended at her elbow.

"True enough. And speaking of which, I did tell everyone to check in on their car radios after Darian came back and took up the bridge watch. Greg had been trying to get ahold of them too. They're all going to clear out once the line of cars passes their positions. After that, they're going to do sweeps of the island, checking for stragglers or signs that people are still in their homes. Somehow, we've kept power this long, so that will help. Next hand."

Rebecca swapped out hands. Once this was all over, she could reward herself with the fragrant broth. "We should give them a call and tell them to stop in and get something to eat and drink before heading out."

"Sounds good. I'm going to grab a bite myself once I'm done with this Florence Nightingale routine."

"Is that going to be anytime soon?" She kept her breathing slow and measured.

"That should do it. But you've got a lot of sand stuck in there. That's probably what's burning so bad."

"What?" Rebecca pulled her hands back and inspected them again. "I already washed them out."

"Tilt them side to side and you can see the shine. Sorry, Boss, but you're going to need a doctor."

"I don't have time for that." She twisted her hands and saw what he was talking about. "We've got about four hours before landfall now."

20

Rebecca sat at her desk, sipping the comforting broth.

"I'm sure there's a ton of other stuff I need to get done too. Hell, I still need someone to drive the whole island with their loudspeaker cranked up, announcing the mandatory evacuation. Plus, I still need to go back to the Munroe house to check over the crime scene."

"What do you need to do that for?" Hoyt used alcohol wipes from the first aid kit to clean the tools he'd used.

"I don't know. Something about the scene downstairs is tickling my brain. I know we've got lots of pictures and video, but standing in the scene makes it more real for me. Easier to put the pieces together."

"I can understand that. And as for the loudspeaker, I can ask Greg to do that. It's damn near impossible to stand upright out there. But he should be able to handle driving through this crap." Her deputy took a big bite of his wife's biscuits and gravy. "I got a text from Ange. She said the Red Cross is set up at the school. People are settling in." Hoyt nudged the wound-cleansing spray toward her.

Rebecca picked it up and applied a liberal amount. "Then what do we do after that?"

"Keep sounding the sirens and conduct basic patrol until it's no longer safe. That's why we weighed down the vehicles first thing. Make sure no one is stuck or lost on the island. Then seek shelter ourselves."

She sighed with relief as the lidocaine in the spray started taking effect. "I'd like to keep one person in the office at all times. Everything we have points at Malcolm Jenner as the killer, but he hasn't been officially charged. It would be best to keep him under watch until everything else is taken care of."

"Ya know," Hoyt smirked as he stood, "you look like a Bond villain sitting there, twisting in your chair while rubbing your hands."

She looked down and saw what he was talking about. "Today, I take over the sheriff's office. Tomorrow, the world!"

They both laughed at her terrible impersonation.

"How about you stick to being sheriff? You'd make a terrible villain."

"You're probably right." Rebecca's mind raced with the list of tasks she needed to complete. "I'm still worried that we haven't gotten in touch with Brady Munroe. Viviane called every number she could find on him. I'm going to head over to the house and see if I can find anything else." She pulled the house keys from the evidence box she still had sitting on her desk.

That little niggling feeling in her mind solidified.

Both the front and back doors were locked. Why? And if Clare was killed in the upstairs bedroom instead of downstairs—and the evidence definitely pointed to that—why were the kitchen and dining room trashed?

"Hold down the fort 'til I get back or someone else comes in. 'Til then, take a break and maybe change into some dry socks. Once you're relieved, start basic patrol patterns. Check up on any stragglers. Whoever comes in next can do the same 'til we've all swapped through."

Hoyt nodded and put away the first aid kit for her as she pulled on her thick, black rubber gloves from her belt pouch. "You going to go get your hands checked?"

She shook her head. "No. I need to confirm that the car that hit that tree is our guy's, then I'm going to check the crime scene. I think we missed something vital."

He frowned, and his eyebrows knit together.

She clarified. "Not we, not you, *me*. I feel like I'm missing something with this case. Maybe it's because I got interrupted and had to run out."

"Okay, whatever floats your boat. And you'll be going right past Greg on your way. How about you let me check on the car while you do the rest?"

"Perfect. I'll make sure to stop and ask him to start driving around and making the evacuation announcement." Now that her hands were cleaned and protected, she grabbed her keys and headed out.

The coat she'd been wearing all day didn't have time to dry in between trips, and it was starting to feel soggy and sticky on the inside. Rebecca prayed the electricity held out long enough for her to finish her work and get a hot shower.

Dreams of a deliciously warm shower and a soft, comfy bed filled her mind as she pulled up next to Greg's position.

Greg's cruiser was where he was supposed to be, but the man himself was not. Rebecca let her foot off the brake and rolled forward, checking both sides of the road.

It had been dark before with the heavy cloud cover. Now, even though the sun should be near its peak in the sky, the island was as dark as a moonless night.

Lightning raked down, lighting up the sky.

Oh, of course. Why wouldn't things get worse? Shit! Is Greg out walking in this?

Pressing down slightly on the accelerator, Rebecca hurried her search. Flipping on her spotlight helped as she waved it back and forth.

Nearly a quarter mile down the road, a light flashed. Then flashed again. A flashlight swinging forward and back.

Rebecca pointed the spotlight there and spotted a dark shape with reflective stripes. Pressing down on the gas, she drove straight for the figure running toward her. The figure left the sidewalk and ran into the street as she got closer. As he passed in front of her car, she saw that it was Greg and unlocked the doors.

"Holy shit!" He gasped as he jumped in and slammed the door shut. "That was close! Thanks for the lift."

"Yes. What were you doing?"

"Thought I heard someone and went to investigate." He shook his head. "Didn't see nothing. What are you doing here? Were you out here looking for me?"

"Checking in on you, yeah. I didn't see the lightning 'til I got here. Has it been doing that for long?" Rebecca peered around, checking for anyone else who might be outside as the weather turned even more dangerous.

"Just long enough for me to run myself ragged." Greg tried to catch his breath as he pulled on his seat belt.

"Anyone else out here? Or do you want to go back to your cruiser?"

"Not a soul I could find. And yeah, my cruiser's just a bit behind us."

Rebecca made a U-turn and headed back to Greg's Explorer. "Well, we need to make sure no one is defying the evacuation order and trying to ride this out by sheltering in place. I need you to drive the island with your loudspeaker blaring and announce the requirement to evacuate. Look for signs of life in any of the homes. If you run across anyone, either tell them to get off the island or head to the shelter at the town hall."

"Yeah, I can do that." He leaned over and grabbed the radio. "Who all has their ears on? Over."

There was a loud crack behind them, and Rebecca's eyes darted up to the rearview mirror. A large, red oak fell into the street, its trunk snapped in half by the strength of the wind.

Her sphincter was getting a workout today.

"Yeah, I'm here, Greg. What's up? Over." Locke's voice came over the radio.

Rebecca felt another chill as she thought about how many people were out on these streets trying to help others get to safety. "Where is he?"

"What's your location, Locke? Over."

"Main Street still. Where'd you think I was? Over."

Greg scowled at the tone. "If there was any justice in the world, you'd be facedown in the sand somewhere you—"

Rebecca snatched the radio from his hands, and Greg clenched his jaw. "Locke, this is West. Stay close to your cruiser. Lightning in the area. As soon as you can see the end of the line of cars, head back to the station. Hoyt will let you know what to do. Over."

When Locke responded, his voice was shaky. "Copy that, Sheriff. Will do. Over."

Driving with one hand wasn't the best idea right now, but Rebecca didn't think giving the radio back to Greg was a good plan either.

"You okay, Greg?"

"I'm fine."

She didn't say anything, and he darted a glance at her before turning back to stare out the window.

"I'm having…a bad day," he muttered into the glass, his breath fogging it up.

"We all have bad days. I understand that." His cruiser came into view. "Why don't you go ahead and evacuate after you drive the streets? You've put in a full day. I don't think we're respecting your retirement very well, eh? Time to relax and kick back someplace warm and dry."

"I'm fine." His sigh was so heavy, it rattled with emotion.

Rebecca could tell he wasn't in the mood for humor.

"Lord help me, I can't forgive that boy. Every damn time an asshole comment comes out of his mouth, I wanna punch it back into his face. Was that the last thing my friend heard before he was gunned down? Did Locke say some shitty thing like that when Wallace was shot? Or did he just step over his body in his race for glory?"

Rebecca had no answer for that. She didn't know, and she'd been there. If Locke had said anything to Wallace, she wouldn't have been able to hear it over the sound of the waves and the conversation she'd been wrapped up in.

"Wallace was never happy about hiring the boy. Did you know that? He was told by the Select Board to hire him. Locke was the only candidate at the time and had a good résumé." He stared out the window. Or maybe he was staring at his own reflection in the glass.

"Really?" Rebecca prompted.

"He was in a rush to hire someone to replace me. Because I wanted to retire and was only working part-time. And while there's definitely been an uptick in crime around here, Locke's the reason I came back to help out, once it was clear he didn't know what the hell he was doing."

"It's not your fault."

"But if I hadn't retired, Locke never would have been hired at all. And I would have been the one watching your back that night with him."

His anger made sense now. And Rebecca made a mental note to research Locke's credentials a little bit deeper. "I'm sorry. I really am."

"Not your fault. None of this was your fault, and you've moved heaven and earth to make things right again."

She stopped next to his SUV, and he unlocked his seat belt. "You okay?"

"Yep. Thanks." His tone was gruff as he got out of her cruiser, but she knew he wasn't just thanking her for the ride. The wind caught the door and blew it fully open.

"Greg." He ducked down to look into the cabin. "It's not my fault. But I am still sorry for your loss."

He bobbed his head. "Me, too, Sheriff. Me too." Using both hands, he leaned hard to close the cruiser's passenger door.

Making another U-turn, Rebecca continued toward the Munroe home. She managed to get Darian on the radio and told him the same thing she'd told Locke, knowing he would be the last one in, as he was set up at the bridge.

Everything that had been said rolled through her mind as she pulled up in front of the crime scene. Pulling out her pocketknife, she sliced through the seal, unlocked the door, and walked into the home once more.

The wind was blowing so hard that it sucked the door closed, ripping the knob from her hands.

"What the hell?"

The winds were reaching levels Rebecca had only ever seen while watching the Weather Channel from the comfort of her couch. Jim Cantore had always preached caution while defying his own instructions and braving the worst weather conditions.

Turning and kneeling, she inspected the doorknob. Fingerprinting powder residue was visible, so she knew Hoyt had processed it. Underneath and around it, she noticed the bloody smears she'd seen her first time through.

"Blood on this doorknob, so obviously someone opened this door with blood on their hands. Maybe they came back in, as well, but the blood was washed off before we got here?" She'd spent long enough on the porch looking for signs of distress that she knew she hadn't missed anything out there.

"But more blood on the carpet, here and here." She walked through the house, talking out loud because the rain was so loud, she couldn't hear herself thinking. "Fight in the breakfast room. Table is moved. And there's a blood pool on the floor. A pool. Not drops, not splatter. But a pool. That means someone stood here with blood pouring down. They bled here."

For the first time, she stepped around it and looked at it from the other side. She had to squat down to figure out what she was seeing. The blood pool was shallower along this edge, like it had soaked into something or been blocked by something porous as the blood poured.

"Those are the shape of shoulders." Rebecca held her hands out in front of her, just inside each line. "Wide shoulders. Probably a man. This wasn't from Clare's attack. Or a spill. Was there another person here?"

She stood and walked to the counter where she'd seen the knife block. The design of the handle matched the one embedded in Clare's chest. But a second knife was missing—a smaller one. When she recalled the wounds she'd measured with Dr. Evan, a smaller knife didn't track with any of Clare's injuries.

She checked the sink and dishwasher. No knife in either place.

Everything she had seen came together, and she moved to the back door, where there was the same bloody smear on the door handle that she'd seen earlier with Hoyt. She placed her hand on the sliding glass, but it wouldn't budge. She flipped the latch and unsealed her deputy's hard work.

It was so dark out that she had to use her flashlight to see the end of the weathered wood that stretched out from the sliding glass door. The back porch was in disrepair and was probably rarely used. That was a shame since it led directly to the beach.

Struggling to keep her eyes open against the harsh, salt-water wind, Rebecca pressed forward. If there had been furniture on the deck, it was gone now, as were any drops of blood she could have collected. The wind screamed, and lightning forked from the sky to the water with a loud crack and pop.

"Shit! This is so stupid."

Rebecca pushed her way out of the house and into the teeth of the storm, looking for a second victim.

21

It didn't take long.

After finding the path to the beach, Rebecca had barely hit the sand when she nearly tripped over a body. Tucked into the dune grasses and slathered in sand, a man she assumed was Brady Munroe didn't move or make a sound when her foot caught on his leg.

After regaining her balance, she knelt and pressed two fingers against his neck, taking in his features. They matched the photo she'd seen earlier. With the roar of the ocean and the pounding of the storm, it was challenging to assess his condition. Holding her breath and focusing all her efforts on the place where her skin pressed against his, she waited.

She felt it!

Faint but definitely there, his pulse tapped against the nitrile covering her fingers.

Scooching closer, she moved over his face to protect it from the elements while she fumbled for her radio. She nearly screamed when his eyes shot open.

"Mer…maid."

At least, that was what she thought he said.

"What? What did you say? Talk to me."

His bloodshot eyes were horrifying. A groan was his only response. Then his eyes fluttered closed. His hand moved to his belly, and when she lifted his rain slicker and shirt to peek underneath, she spotted the point of his distress.

Blood oozed down his side.

"Brady. Hold on. I'm going to get you help."

Rebecca pressed her gloved fingers into the side of his neck again. Still faint and thready. Pulling out her radio, she lifted his shirt and winced at the stab wound halfway down his side.

She keyed the radio and called in their situation and location, then waited for almost a full minute for a reply.

"Copy that."

Rebecca recognized the voice of Sandra Baker and sagged in relief.

"It'll take us at least thirty minutes to get to your location. We're on the north side of the island and have a downed tree blocking our path. Over."

Thirty minutes?

She didn't know if Brady had that long. And she certainly didn't want to sit out in these elements any longer than necessary.

"Copy that. I'm going to try to get him to my cruiser. Will let you know if I succeed. Over."

"Good luck, Sheriff. We'll be there as quick as we can. Over."

Cursing under her breath, Rebecca pulled off her coat and laid it next to Brady. She needed to put pressure on the wound but decided getting out of the storm was paramount. With the coat beside him, she carefully rolled him onto his side. Reaching across his body, she stuffed as much of the coat under him as she could.

"I could use a little assistance right about now," she muttered.

Brady didn't reply. He was no longer conscious. His eyelids didn't even flutter, but when she checked his pulse again, it was still there.

Stepping back to catch her breath, her foot caught on something, nearly tripping her.

It was the wooden handle of a knife.

If she hadn't been out in the middle of a hurricane, she would have changed gloves before handling the weapon. Under current conditions, though, she slipped it into an evidence bag as carefully as she could.

How had it gotten there?

Had Brady removed it from his gut and brought it with him? Why? Self-defense? Had he feared his assailant would return to finish him off? Or had the knife still been buried in his flesh and only come free when he collapsed?

Oh God. His assailant.

She'd left Jenner in an open room. Was he roaming the streets right then?

One thing at a time. She'd have to worry about that later.

With no other way to carry it, she rolled the knife in the bag until the plastic formed a thin barrier around the blade. She then tucked it next to Munroe before securing the sleeves of her rain slicker around his arms to give her a handle of sorts with which to pull him.

She covered his face the best she could from the elements. Death by drowning in the rain would have been a concept she'd have scoffed at until today. Now, seeing him prone in this downpour, she thought it was an absolute possibility.

Let's go.

It was a struggle to get him moving, but it became easier once she had some momentum. Except for the wet sand, which seemed to want to hold on to him and kept shifting under her feet.

Feeling a bit of firmness, she looked behind her as she took her second backward step onto the grass. Her footing was just as slippery as it had been in the sand, but at least the raincoat slid over it with less friction.

She was soaked through, her hair hanging forward in her face as the heavy, wet locks pulled at her hair tie, fighting to keep them contained. Her hands cramped—at least she could feel them—and her shoulder screamed as she continued to strain against the pull. A tree branch smacked her back.

"Shit." She hissed as another one landed a few feet away. Pausing, she flipped over the side of the coat to cover Brady's face again. It would be a complete kick in the teeth to have him drown while being rescued.

A shredded palm tree branch slashed down just over her head. Ducking, she looked up as the tree swayed and let out a loud, ominous creak.

"Crap!"

Keeping low, she turned and lurched forward, and again, gripping the coat with her left hand. At least the wind was at her back, practically pushing her away from the ocean. Would it be enough?

The creaking got louder, interrupted by several loud snaps and pops. When the tree swayed back and forth in the wind before breaking free in the gale, adrenaline flooded Rebecca's system, giving her the extra strength to run. The pops turned to crackles as the branches of the large tree snapped and started falling right toward them.

Rebecca continued to run for her cruiser, dragging some two-hundred-odd pounds behind her like it was nothing. It was parked at the end of the yard, so she only had to cross the lawn. She refused to look back as the sounds got louder, and the ground shook under her feet.

It wasn't until she reached the cruiser that she finally dared a glance. The palm tree's glorious crown lay only a couple of yards from where she stood.

"Shit. Shit. Shit."

As quickly as she could, she opened the back door. The wind pulled it the rest of the way open, holding it wide. She prayed the gusts didn't turn and slam it shut on her as she dropped to her knees to grab Brady's limp arm and pull it over her shoulder. Grabbing his waistband, she lifted him in a fireman's carry. His weight threatened to buckle her knees, but she worked past the strain.

Turning, she managed to get him seated sideways in the back seat. Once his center of gravity was settled, she lowered the rest of his torso in, screaming as her back protested the maneuver. Once all his weight was off her shoulders, she ran around the SUV and pulled him the rest of the way in.

His rain slicker and shirt had slipped up his back from the fireman's carry, exposing his wound, which started leaking again. Yanking the sleeves of her raincoat around him, she tied the arms as tight as she could over the injury.

The knife had landed on the floorboard, and she left it there for now. There was no way for her to do more, even if she had the time. Once Brady was all the way in, she slammed the door shut and, once again, ran around the cruiser.

Movement in the yard caught her attention. The wind rocked another palm tree back and forth like a pendulum. This one was even closer to where she was parked. She kept her eyes on it as she slammed the other back seat door, jumped into the front seat, and hit reverse.

As fast as was safe, she backed away from the house, turning to get out of the tree's trajectory should it be lifted aloft. With the way this day was going, it wouldn't surprise her.

Glancing back, she could just barely see the victim's face. He was unresponsive. His breathing was shallow and slow. A gray pallor covered every visible part of his body.

Since they still had no time of death for Clare or any idea how long Jenner had wandered free before reaching the station, there was no telling how long he'd been bleeding out on the beach. Or how much longer he had before he ran out of blood. Rebecca had witnessed death, and her experience told her Brady Munroe didn't have much time.

With trembling hands, she radioed the paramedics and the health center, letting them know she was en route.

While the flooding on the evacuation route had been taken care of, those were not the roads she needed to drive now. Floodwater ran down the lawns of neighboring houses. The volume, speed, and duration of the rain meant the storm drains couldn't keep up. Trash, toys, and storm debris clogged the drains, exacerbating the problem.

She had to swerve several times to avoid the deeper waters cresting the curbs. Which was still better than when she had to swerve as shutters, branches, and trash cans were either already in the road or thrown at her like urban projectiles.

The smaller things she didn't bother to avoid because that would have resulted in her swerving the entire trip. Instead, she flinched as things too small and too fast to see pinged off her windshield.

Her breathing was heavy, her knuckles were white, and her hands throbbed as she fought against the raging wind to steer her way to the health center. Seeing lights inside the building made her sigh with relief. More than a few of the streetlights she'd passed had been out. Perhaps they'd switched to using backup generators? She couldn't be sure until she got inside.

There were few cars in the parking lot, most people

having heeded the evacuation order. She had plenty of room to maneuver as she pulled as close to the side door as she could get. Hitting her siren for a few beats, she prayed someone would hear it.

She threw the car into park and muscled open the door. A nurse was outside before she could get out of the vehicle.

"What've you got?" the nurse yelled as she yanked the back door open.

Rebecca cupped her hands around her mouth to explain. "Male, forty-five years of age, deep stab wound in the upper right-hand quadrant of the abdominal cavity. He's lost a lot of blood."

Another nurse came out with a gurney. Rebecca stepped back to let the professionals take over, relegating her role to holding the door open as the wind kept trying to slam it closed.

Working together, the women smoothly and efficiently slipped Munroe out of the car and onto the gurney. They didn't need her help. So once they had him safely inside, she picked up the knife—glad to see it hadn't poked through the evidence bag—and darted indoors.

Dr. Evan was turning into a room as Rebecca burst through the doors. The doctor paused, her gaze dropping to the knife.

"Is that what caused the wound?"

"It was close to where I found him, so I think so." Rebecca rushed over to show it to her. "I'm not sure if he pulled it out or carried it with him. Hell, considering what's raging outside, I wouldn't be surprised if the wind had torn it free."

"Let me see."

She held the knife up while the doctor inspected it through the bag. "Smooth. Kitchen knife. Fine point. About six inches. Any chance you know how deep it went in? It could help us save him." Dr. Evan turned and entered the exam room.

Rebecca followed her. "Sadly, no. There's no blood left on it. The sand and rain took it all."

The nurses were cutting Brady Munroe's shirt off. Dr. Evan went to wash her hands.

"Well, kitchen knife wounds are what I usually see. Just not in this position. Was he awake?"

"He opened his eyes once. Managed to say just one word before he lost consciousness." Rebecca stepped to the side, setting herself up in the corner. "His name is Brady Munroe."

Dr. Evan's head jerked around. "Clare's husband? Does he know?"

"Clare?" a man's voice croaked out.

Both doctor and sheriff moved closer to him.

"Mr. Munroe, can you tell me what happened to you?"

At the doctor's question, his eyes struggled to open. "Clare? She's..." Tears slid down his temples. "Catch him. You...you have to catch him."

22

There were sixty-four ceiling tiles in the examination room. One had a chip in the corner. Another sported a faint crack. Yet another had a dark splotch that Rebecca wasn't sure was water damage or bodily fluid she didn't want to consider.

She knew every detail about the room because she inspected it as a nurse abraded her hands. She barely refrained from cursing as iodine was forced into her wounds.

Damn Dr. Evan.

It had been the doctor who'd noticed the shape of Rebecca's hands through the torn gloves she was still wearing.

After insisting she take them off, Dr. Evan demanded her palms be examined.

So here she was, counting ceiling tiles while a demon nurse cleaned her wounds. Brady Munroe was in surgery, so it wasn't like she could question him. But still…

It wasn't just painful. It was also disconcerting. Even with the numbing spray, she could swear she felt every bristle as it passed over her hands. Her stomach twisted and writhed with the feeling. Maybe she should just give up eating for the rest of the day. At least that would calm down one part of her body.

The nurse patted her knee. "We're nearly finished, Sheriff."

Foolishly, Rebecca looked down and saw the nurse pick up the bottle of iodine again. Her gaze shot back up to the ceiling.

"Are you squeamish about the sight of blood?" The nurse's tone was friendly enough, but there was a hint of disbelief in it.

"Not at all, um…" She scanned her scrubs for a name tag.

"Denise."

Rebecca smiled despite the discomfort. "I don't think I could do my job if that were the case, Denise. But it's like a papercut or a razor nick. It doesn't really hurt so long as you don't look at it."

The tugging started again as the nurse continued to remove splinters. "Ah. That's very smart, then. These hands are badly swollen. How long ago did this happen?"

"Oh, about eight emergencies ago. I'm not really sure anymore."

"I get ya. It's been a crazy day here too. Those emergencies explain how you got so much packed into your hands. There're fibers, sand, and I think some salt and plastic too."

Cool liquid ran over her raw flesh as her wounds were rinsed.

"We're almost done, though. Then we can get you wrapped up. You should start feeling better almost immediately, now that we've got everything out of them."

Soft gauze was pressed against her hands, but Rebecca kept her eyes averted.

"Will the swelling go down?"

"That depends. If you keep irritating them, then no. If you

can keep your hands off things, then yes. Try to limit the amount of tight gripping you do. And of course, try to keep from handling rough items as well. Keeping them dry is also important."

Unable to help herself, she looked Denise in the eyes and laughed. "So no more hauling bodies off the beach? Or stacking sandbags? Or working in the rain?"

Denise chuckled. "I'll glue the worst of the wounds, then secure finger cots for protection."

Rebecca thought about it. She hoped she didn't need to use her gun at any point in the near future. But if she did, the nurse's strategy should allow her finger to access the trigger guard.

"That should work. Thanks."

"I'll load you up with some additional cots and bandages in case you need them later. And if worse comes to worst, come back here, and I'll rebandage you." There was respect and compassion in the woman's dark eyes. "I know you guys are running lean. There's a few of us staying behind, so don't hesitate to let us know if we can help."

Worry sawed across Rebecca's mind, its razor-sharp teeth digging deep. She knew emergency personnel of all kinds made sacrifices during times like these, but she didn't like it. "You've got a safe place to go?"

"We'll be fine. How about you?"

The radio by her side crackled. "Sheriff West, come in." It was a male voice, but she didn't recognize it through the static.

"Duty calls." Denise frowned at the device. "Can anyone else answer it?"

"I'm the only one, I'm afraid." Rebecca tried to reach for the radio, but Denise's grip tightened.

"Just a little bit more."

A minute later, her hands cleaned and secured, Rebecca

keyed the radio's mic and walked toward the front of the building, where reception was better. "Sheriff West here. Go ahead. Over."

"Rebecca? I have a bit of a situation here."

It was Ryker Sawyer. Her heart rate kicked up.

"Here? As in, on the island? You were supposed to evacuate. How come you haven't? Over."

"I was on my way to do just that when I swung by to check on my neighbors. They're getting on in age and sometimes need help with things. I wanted to make sure they were all loaded up and prepared. Oh, and over."

In the background, Rebecca heard an elderly woman's voice raised in anger and fear, but she couldn't make out the words.

"Copy that. I take it the neighbors need help? Over."

"Mr. Pranger left nearly two hours ago to get batteries for the flashlights but hasn't come back. He's not answering his phone either. And their car is still in the driveway. Over."

"Old fool walked to the store because he said it would be faster!" The woman was clearer now, as was the panic in her voice. "I told him we didn't need flashlights if we got to the mainland. But he swore they would lose power, too, and didn't want to be caught without a light source. His eyesight isn't what it used to be, especially in the dark."

Rebecca closed her eyes. "Ryker, how old is Mr. Pranger? Over."

He relayed her question, then a quavering voice answered so softly she couldn't make it out.

"He's eighty-three," Ryker repeated. "And they've lived here for more than sixty years now. He knows every shortcut and path in this town. That's why he thought he could walk to the store with no problem and make it back. But there's no way he should have been gone this long. Over."

"He's eighty-three, can barely see, and he's out in this?

Holy shit, Ryker, a tree limb could have taken him down. Over."

"I know. That's why I called you. We have to find him. Can you drive over here and help me search? Over."

"Of course. Over."

After Ryker rattled off the Prangers' address, a hand grabbed her arm. It was Denise holding a plastic bag filled with supplies.

Rebecca mouthed a *thank you.*

Denise didn't release her. "I couldn't help overhearing. Once you find Mr. Pranger, bring him here for a checkup. His eyesight isn't the only thing that's weak."

With those words of warning, Rebecca grabbed her things and ran back into the storm.

23

"Who has their ears on?" Rebecca asked as soon as she got back into the Explorer. Without her raincoat, she was drenched and chilled. The engine was still warm when she turned it on, so hot air blew out, thankfully.

"I'm here, Sheriff," Locke responded. "What ya need? Over."

Rebecca pulled out of the parking lot and headed east. "I just got a call for a possible silver alert. Eighty-three-year-old male tried to walk to a nearby store and hasn't been heard from for more than two hours. Last name Pranger. First name Clarence. Over."

"Copy that, Sheriff," Hoyt said. "I know Clarence and Edith. He had to walk because he lost his license six months ago after failing the vision test. Over."

Living in such a small town did have its advantages. "Copy that. Which of you are at the station?"

"I am." Strangely, Locke's voice was devoid of anger or derision. "And yeah, Clarence's eyesight is total crap, especially in low light. He wears thick glasses too. That's really going to mess him up in this rain. I can get in the cruiser and go searching for him."

"Is Jenner still there? How's he doing? Over."

"He's..." Locke sighed. "He's mumbling to himself almost nonstop. I can't make anything out, though. Just talking about mermaids and nets and weird shit."

Rebecca cursed as she tightened her sore hands on the wheel when the wind buffeted the Explorer, shaking it back and forth. She could only imagine what the weather would be doing to a frail body caught out in it. As much as she wanted to race to the scene, that would be both reckless and useless. After all, she would be driving through the area where Mr. Pranger had gone missing.

"If Jenner's talking at all, maybe he's coming around. I found another stabbing victim, Brady Munroe. He's at the health center now, getting treated."

"That explains why he wasn't answering our calls," Hoyt said. "Where was Clarence heading? The hardware store?"

Rebecca turned on her searchlight, hunching over the steering wheel as she juggled the radio and tried to get the light pointed at the same time. "Yeah. How'd you know?"

"He always stocks up on batteries when bad weather comes in. He must have a warehouse of his own by now, but he swears you need fresh batteries each time. Sheriff, I'll head to the hardware store first if you want to go talk with Edith and start from that side. Over."

"Ten-four. Ryker did say he knows all the shortcuts in the area and uses them frequently, so check yards as well. Over."

"He knows those shortcuts because he made them." Locke chuckled. "Back when he was a teacher, he'd take us out on 'educational hikes' and teach us about plants and animals and even electricity and...." His voice trailed off, and when it came back, it was filled with concern. "Sheriff, you gotta find him. That man's a treasure. We can't lose him. Over."

"I'm halfway there, Locke. I'll do my best. What can you tell me about those hikes? Over."

"He went all over the island, but we always started from the school and ended in a field of some kind. Or marsh or copse of trees. I know he had other trails he used, but I don't know how to find them if they started at his house. Over."

"Tell me about the trails, Locke. Spots he avoided, areas he was attracted to. Over." She peered out into the dark, trying to catch sight of anything moving. The problem was that everything was moving. Trash cans rocketed through the air. Water rushed through gutters. Trees, bushes, and grass bent in the wind. All of it made a perfect camouflage for a man standing or lying on the ground.

"Sorry, Sheriff. I don't think those will help. He made those trails just for us. For the students, the kids. They avoided houses and businesses. He didn't want us to get in trouble and said those were the best areas to find wildlife too. Over."

It had been worth a shot. "Copy. I'm pulling up to their house now. Hoyt, you keep searching. I'm going to ask Edith if she knows any of his trails. Over."

"Roger that, Boss. Over."

"Locke, I need you at the station. Malcolm Jenner, coherent or not, is the closest thing we've got to a suspect in a murder and attempted-murder investigation. Over."

"You got it, Sheriff. Over."

It wasn't until Rebecca pulled into the address Ryker had given her that she realized he might have told her the wrong numbers. His truck sat in the driveway, and his last name was spelled out in block letters on the porch.

So...did the Prangers live on his left or right?

Neither house had lights showing through the windows, but Ryker's did. She reached into the door panel and grabbed another handheld spotlight stored there.

Rebecca pushed out of her cruiser and her breath was stolen from her lungs. If she struggled to take in air, what would an elderly man do in these conditions?

She ran up to Ryker's door, pounding on it without thinking. The pounding was a bad plan and set her hand screaming all over again.

Ryker must have been waiting since the door opened so fast. "Come in."

Rebecca stepped inside, and he slammed the door shut against the steady onslaught of rain that had already soaked through the towels he'd laid out in the tiled entryway.

"Don't you have a coat? What the hell, Rebecca?"

"Ryker, don't talk like that to her. Go get her a fresh towel." Edith Pranger scowled at the younger man as she shuffled forward. "Dear, you need to be wearing a coat in this kind of weather."

Surprised at the direction the conversation was taking, Rebecca nodded. "Had one on all day, until I had to use it to save another man's life. Haven't had time to grab a spare."

Edith stepped forward and started fussing over Rebecca, brushing her hair back with twisted, pale fingers. "Oh, you poor, sweet dear. Would you like to borrow mine? I won't need it 'til you get back. I'm not going anywhere without my husband." Her hands continued to brush the water off Rebecca's arms as she turned to face Ryker, who was coming back holding a thick beach towel.

"Ryker, boy, where did I put my rain jacket? This young lady needs to borrow it for a bit."

Ryker wrapped the towel around Rebecca, squeezing it tight as he stared at her bandaged hands.

Seeing where he was looking, she shrugged and started drying herself with the oversized rainbow towel. "Long story for another time. I've been told Clarence liked to make his own paths to get around town. I assume he used them often, and even more since he lost his license?"

Edith nodded. "Yes, he would walk straight out the door, then veer a bit left when he got across the street. I know he ducked between a shrub and the Smiths' house, but I never followed, so I don't know where he went from there."

"Ryker, do you know?"

"He showed me a path to the Blackwelders' back door once, when we were looking for their lost cat. That goes along the same direction."

"Think you could find it again?"

"I can give it my best shot."

Rebecca took the opportunity while they were talking to remove the stretched-out band from her hair and try to pull it back again. With the thick towel wrapped around her shoulders, it wasn't easy, and it almost certainly wasn't pretty, but she got it done.

She was a bedraggled mess.

And Ryker looked so good.

What the hell?

She ran through a practiced list of reasons why her line of thinking was self-destructive and a pointless waste of time. Her appearance and Ryker's assessment of it didn't matter. Clarence Pranger was what mattered.

"Let's start there, then. Once I'm on the path, I might be able to follow it to wherever he went missing." Squeezing the towel against her sopping clothing one last time, she handed the wet cloth to Ryker.

He dropped it on the floor. "What's this *I* business?" He reached out and pulled a strip of palm leaf from her hair. "I'm going with you. Two people can search faster, and I do have some experience following Clarence's trails."

"She can't go out like this again. Maybe one of your dry shirts. That would be the gentlemanly thing to do. And then give her my raincoat." Edith wrapped her thin arms around Rebecca's shoulders. "Oh, you're already chilled too. Water makes you lose your body heat faster. You're going to catch a cold. Ryker, maybe you should go alone."

Ryker raced off and was back in a flash with a t-shirt.

Rebecca slipped into the next room for a quick change and was back in a snap, too, before she even had time to consider how intimate it was that she was wearing something of his.

Ryker was pulling his jacket on. Raising an eyebrow at her in his shirt, he opened his mouth to comment, but she cut him off.

"I've got the big light and the radio," Rebecca pointed out. "And my men are already out looking for him too. By the hardware store."

Edith's face dissolved into lines of worry as Ryker picked up a large flashlight. "Okay, then I'll make you something warm to eat while you're gone. Oh, do you drink coffee?"

"Yes, please, ma'am." Rebecca's mood brightened at the thought. She couldn't even remember where she'd left her last cup, things had been so hectic today. She also couldn't remember the last time she'd been fussed over so much.

"I'll put the pot on. And get some towels for Clarence when he gets back." Edith nodded as if things were settled.

"Just help yourself, Edith. You know where everything is."

Rebecca lifted an eyebrow. "Oh really? Does Edith come over quite a bit?"

He grinned. "Don't you want to know?"

Actually, she did. She wanted to know much more about this man, but learning he was shagging his senior neighbor wasn't what she had in mind. Not that she thought their relationship was anything but innocent.

Ryker pulled a coat from the rack behind the door. It was

bright yellow with little orange duckies and a floppy hood—the cherry on top of her wounded pride over her appearance.

"This should cap off the ensemble." Ryker gave her a wink.

"Thank you so much, Mrs. Pranger." She smiled as she pulled on the vibrant rain slicker.

"Please, dear, call me Edith. And it's the least I can do for someone trying to save my husband. I'll go see about that coffee now."

The elderly woman turned away, heading for the kitchen, and began praying out loud. "Heavenly Father, I ask that you protect my husband from his own foolish ways and look over these two young ones as they work to keep his bony ass safe."

Rebecca pressed her lips together to keep from giggling before heading out the door.

Ryker didn't hesitate as they walked out into the shrieking tempest with his run-of-the-mill flashlight lighting their path. He crossed the street, moving slowly and keeping his head down. The harsh wind was coming in at their backs for the most part, so at least they didn't have to fight against it yet.

He led her to the corner of a house and disappeared. Rebecca moved forward and turned on her light. Ryker's arm reached out from a break in the bushes, showing her the way. Following his lead, she stepped into a natural hollow that ran another thirty or so feet. It was only wide enough for them to walk single file.

"The wind isn't as strong in here. The plants seem to lessen the effect of the tempest." She motioned him forward, keeping the light in her hand pointed at his feet and away from his eyes.

They walked through the brush, but the branches

thrashed back and forth, beating them from every side and grabbing at their clothes.

Okay, she'd concede it wasn't a perfect shelter, but at least the rain wasn't blowing her off her feet. She focused on Ryker to make sure she didn't lose him.

He moved his mouth close to her ear. "I don't know where to go from here."

"Then let's spread out a bit. Which way is the store?"

Ryker turned in a circle. "That way, I think."

"So we head that way." She stepped up beside him and kept her head down, looking for any tracks or signs of a path. "Use your light to get my attention if you find anything. I'll do the same." They split up to look for any sign of the elderly man.

24

Ryker may have nodded, but Rebecca didn't notice as she headed off to the right of where he'd pointed. If she was where she thought, then the road was just to her right. Even with her powerful light, she couldn't see the houses she knew had to be in that direction.

In fact, it might have been a hindrance as the light reflected on the thick rain that surrounded them like a constantly moving kaleidoscope of gray and white.

It appeared they were in a backyard, one with a row of myrtle trees. There weren't any of the crisp flower petals scattered on the ground like there normally were. And the flat bark on the roots of the tree was shiny and slick under her feet. It took another four steps before she actually saw the trees and the tiny path that wove its way through them.

"This way!" Her voice was taken by the wind, so she swung her light back and forth in the direction Ryker had taken.

His light swung back in response, and he headed her way.

She waited until he was close enough to see, then started

following the path she'd found. Taking it slowly, she checked between each tree, just in case Clarence had fallen.

The path swerved to the left, departing from the grove of trees. Rebecca hesitated. The downtrodden strip she'd been following could have been an animal track, but so could the patchy line that branched back into the trees.

Ryker moved up behind her. "What's wrong?"

"I'm not sure which way to go."

He leaned over her shoulder, following her light as she swung it to the clearer trail out of the trees, then back to the less obvious trail that followed them. "I don't know. Either one is possible. His shortcuts aren't always obvious."

She got on her toes to get close to his ear. "You go left, I'll go straight. Point your light at me every three steps and stop when you can't see me anymore. Radio if you spot him."

The hurricane had finally crippled Rebecca's freakishly good cell service, and she prayed the radios held up during the storm.

Rebecca took another step forward, and Ryker veered off to the side.

She'd only signaled Ryker twice before his light swung over to her and kept shaking. A signal that he'd found something. Her radio crackled.

"Found him."

Turning around wasn't easy on the tight trail she'd been following. Her feet slid on the layers of smooth roots. She grabbed hold of the closest branch and swung around it instead. The thin branch swayed with her added weight, but these trees were used to dealing with everything the ocean could throw at them.

Rebecca didn't want to think about what kind of condition the old man was in after being stuck in the growing maelstrom for the last two hours.

Ducking low and stepping high, she moved toward

where Ryker had disappeared. A man was laid out on the slope just downhill from the path. It looked like he hadn't fallen over so much as slid down the hill. Clarence Pranger was on his side, facing away from her, and holding tightly to something in the ground. From the knees down, he was mired in mud.

But he was moving. Waving at them.

Ryker slid down the gentle slope. Rebecca followed. At least the rain would rinse all the mud off her later.

"I'm s-s-so s-sorry. I f-fell and got s-stuck in the mud when I tried to c-climb out." Mr. Pranger's teeth chattered so hard she was surprised they didn't crack.

"No worries, Mr. Pranger," Ryker yelled. "Accidents happen."

"Hoyt, do you copy? We've found Mr. Pranger. He's alive and alert. Over." Rebecca could only hope her deputy could hear her. The antenna on her handheld wasn't very strong, and it needed the booster from the cruiser to reach longer distances.

No response.

"Careful, Edith!" Clarence cried out as she moved closer. "That path isn't as sturdy as it looks."

"That's not Edith. That's the sheriff." Ryker was on his knees, his flashlight pointed so they could see as much of the area as possible. "We're going to have to dig him out."

Of course they would.

With a sigh, Rebecca went down onto her belly. The mud and water instantly seeped between the snaps of Edith's raincoat.

"Sheriff Wallace? What are you doing out here?"

She patted his ice-cold hand. "I'm Sheriff West, Mr. Pranger. I'll pull you up while Ryker digs, okay?" She said the words with confidence, but she honestly wasn't sure if she would be able to. Her shoulder was already a mess, and her right arm was starting to feel weak. Her hands weren't much better.

"Be careful. If you stick to the grass instead of the reeds, it will work better. The grass might be sharp, but their roots are solid." He pointed to where he clung. "It's the only thing that kept me from slipping down even farther."

Rebecca lifted herself up and checked where she was lying. There was a tuft of grass to her right, so she shifted into a seated position with the grass between her thighs. It should serve as an anchor point, allowing her to still reach the old man.

Ryker dug until one of Pranger's legs freed.

Rebecca grabbed the man by the armpits and pulled.

Nothing.

An eternity later, his other leg was free. She pulled again but barely moved him more than an inch before he cried out in pain.

Ryker weaved his fingers together to form a makeshift stirrup. "Clarence, put your foot in my hands and push when I tell you to."

Pranger shifted to the side and got his foot in Ryker's palms. "Okay."

"On three, the sheriff will pull while you and I push." He met Rebecca's gaze, and she nodded. "One...two...three!"

With all the energy left in her, Rebecca pulled, but even with all their effort, they'd only hauled Pranger a few inches.

"Now your other foot."

Clarence shifted the other way, and they went through the same process. Rebecca adjusted her grip, hooking her arms under his armpits. The shift made a world of difference.

With Ryker pushing and her pulling, they were able to drag Mr. Pranger out of the mud and onto slightly more stable ground.

Once he was safe, Rebecca turned back and reached a hand down to Ryker. Gritting her teeth against the pain she knew was coming, she closed her hand around his wrist while he did the same to her.

"One...two...three!"

She wasn't sure which was going to give out first, her hand or the ground crumbling beneath her.

"Stop being such a gentleman and just climb, dammit!"

He stared at her. "What?" He'd been trying to grab onto any stable part of the hill he could find with his other hand, but the plants kept ripping free, and he couldn't make any progress.

"I'm going to fall if you don't get up here soon! Use me to climb." She shifted until she was on her belly again, her toes dug into the earth for added leverage.

He dropped his head, then lunged upward and grabbed onto her shoulder. She had to dig her knees in to keep from sliding as Ryker scrambled up her body. She grabbed onto any piece of clothing she could get her hands on to help. Something thick splatted onto her cheek, and she squeezed her eyes closed to keep the mud from getting in.

Finally, Ryker was on relatively safe ground beside her. "That was fun."

She was about to respond when several cracks of lightning lit up the sky. She froze, knowing what it meant. This was the outer band of the hurricane.

"Let's get the hell out of here!" Ryker yelled, taking her hand and hauling her up.

She snatched her light. "Good idea. Where's your flashlight?"

He looked down the hill. "Gone."

She nodded in response. "Back the way we came?"

"It's the only way I'm sure will be safe."

This time, Rebecca led the way, as she was the only one

with a light. They moved slowly, holding hands, not just to keep close to each other but to keep Clarence on his feet as well. Lying in the mud had stolen the warmth from his legs, stiffening his muscles and making it difficult to walk. And his glasses needed mini wipers to be of any use. But at least he still had them.

By the time they made it back to the house, most of the mud that coated them and their gear was rinsed clean off, thanks to the battering rain. Silver lining.

They made a sorry sight as they walked through Ryker's front door, but Edith cheered anyway. She had been standing in the entryway, holding a blanket. She dropped the blanket to the floor—gasping when she saw her husband—and stumbled forward to wrap him in a hug.

Seeing that much love and devotion made Rebecca smile. A pang of loneliness and loss gripped her heart as she imagined her parents would have acted much the same way.

As Edith removed Clarence's glasses and wiped them down, Rebecca picked up the blanket and wrapped it around the old man's shoulders. "We need to head to the health center."

"I think I'd like a warm shower first." Clarence's teeth chattered loudly.

Edith handed Clarence's glasses back to him. "And I've got coffee ready for all of you. I'm about to start cooking."

The wind outside shrieked and rattled the windows.

"I'm sorry, but we don't have time. You both need to come with me now. Hurricane Boris is almost here."

25

Clare danced on the beach. Her arms trailed through the air, following her movements as she spun on the toes of one foot. Bending at the waist, her long, shapely leg came up behind her. Her hands brushed the air sinuously as they came down, skimming the white crests of the waves that gently glided around her feet. Streams of her hair caught the golden sun as they steamed over her lithe form, forming gilded streamers that wrapped her elegance in luxury.

When she spotted me watching her, the love in her eyes made the breath catch in my chest. Ruby red lips pulled up into a dazzling smile as she twisted to the side. Finishing her turn, her leg came down, and she started spinning on that foot. Dancing and spinning on the waves and following them out.

Tears prickled my eyes. I adored her. Every move was magic to me. They called to me. Like a siren's call, I could not resist it.

Without thought or hesitation, I took a step toward her. Water splashed over my foot, but I ignored it. I took another step, and the water lapped around my knees. My gaze was focused on Clare as she continued to dance on the waves.

Her smile caught me up again as she turned, silver in her hair.

I stared at the silver and saw it was ephemeral strands of seaweed entwined in her locks. Soaked with water, they caught the light of the moon and seemed to glow with a heavenly light.

Moon? But the sun was just shining. Are the moon and sun in the sky?

That made perfect sense, and I smiled.

She was my sun and my moon. The mystery and allure of the ocean. The grace and beauty of the reeds bending in the wind. She was all that was perfect in the world.

Sure. Loving. Graceful. Kind. Accepting. Beautiful. Forgiving.

The waves breached higher, wrapping her thighs in muddy gray water.

My lips twisted out of their smile. The water touching her was dirty. But she didn't seem to care. Clare continued to dance along the ocean's surface.

I leaned forward, having to push with my arms to get through the water, which was all that kept us apart. My next step met with nothing. The sand had fallen away. I swam, stroking my arms and kicking my feet.

Clare turned and spun, pushing off into a graceful leap. Her arms reached to the sun as the moon shone along her back and legs. She leaped so high, I thought she had taken flight.

This was it. She was going back to the heavens from which she had descended.

"Clare!" My voice was so harsh, angry, cruel—I almost didn't recognize it.

She faltered in her jump and spun from me.

"You can't leave me!" My anger poured out, and I swam faster, trying to reach her. To stop her from escaping. She was mine, and I couldn't let her go.

She was ripped from the sky. Her body propelling to the earth without thought or care.

I watched as her foot slammed into the water. She crumpled, her body collapsing in slow motion. Clare's hair spilled over, covering her body and hiding it from my sight.

The ephemeral seaweed slopped against her head, becoming solid and heavy. It weighed her down, turning to pulp and painting her in a soggy mess.

That's when I heard a sound I didn't recognize.

It was a broken sob, filled with agony and hopelessness.

A sound I'd only ever heard in movies. Such a sound did not make sense in real life. Indeed, it made no sense coming from my Clare. She was always filled with happy sounds. Laughter, joy, animated talking, singing. Those were the sounds my Clare produced.

Slowly, her head lifted. On shaky arms, she pushed herself up and out of the shallow water. She was folded in half, her chest lying over her twisted tail. Her fins twitched in pain, and she stared at me in shock.

This isn't right. This can't be right. I would never do that to her. Would I?

My arms continued to move, taking me closer to where she lay, even as I recoiled in disgust.

Crimson spilled out of her chest as she struggled to rise again. Her tail was weak and wouldn't hold her body up.

I had to help. But for some reason, I couldn't swim straight. Something was pulling at me, keeping me away from her.

It wasn't fair! I'd won her, and she'd promised to always stay with me.

My arms felt strange, and I stared down at them.

The knife I clutched in my hand glittered in the moonlit sea, shining with a ruby hue that spread through the water. Like the fires of Hell, it spread around me. Wider and wider, it moved until it encircled Clare's collapsed form.

She lifted her head, and her eyes widened as she stared at me. The love left her eyes. The shine faded. Sand was crusted on her hands as she lifted them shakily to her chest. They clutched at the hole where her heart had once been.

I could see straight through her to the dark sky at her back. Blood oozed down thickly from the tunnel burrowing between her breasts.

"How could you?" she croaked in pain, making me flinch. Blood bubbled from her mouth. Her eyes turned dull, dead, and unseeing. Her tail stopped twitching, then rotted away, leaving a decomposing stump where her hips had been.

"Clare!" I sobbed, seeing what I'd done to my love. In trying to keep her with me, I'd destroyed her forever.

"I didn't mean to. I didn't want this."

My beloved's body dissolved into the sea. It bubbled as it turned to a slurry of dirty sea-foam.

I stared at the bloody knife in my hands as sand stretched out around me. There was no hint of water in sight. The sun glared down at me, burning my flesh. Heat shimmered all around, distorting my view, and I couldn't tell where I was. Harsh winds shrieked and screamed as they blazed past.

There were sounds, loud and repetitive all around, but I couldn't make out what they were. They beat against my crackling skin, painful and intrusive. I tried to push them away, to focus, but I couldn't find the strength.

What am I doing? Where am I? What have I done?

I stared around again, trying to figure out what had happened.

Where did she go? How could she just leave me like this?

Searing pain in the palms of my hands made me look down.

The blade of the knife had pierced both of them, binding them together. I tried to pull them apart, but it was like ripping off my own arm. Horror filled me, and I struggled to free my hands of each other.

This couldn't be real. I hadn't done this. But it was right there in front of me, right where I could see it. I couldn't look away. The blade was in my hands! *It was right there for anyone to see!*

I had to get rid of it.

With a cry of pain and loss, I pulled, tearing my hands apart and exposing the sharp-edged metal that stretched between them, coated in my fresh blood.

The blade turned to rust and crumbled as it fell from my hands like grains from an hourglass. The reddish fragments blew across the sand, staining it as the wind mixed them together.

I refocused and flipped my hands over and over. They were clean now. There wasn't even a wound.

No wounds. I hadn't done it. The proof was right in front of my eyes. The knife was gone. No one had seen it. Nothing was left.

Relieved, I lifted my eyes. The ocean and the sand were gone. I was in a room. Blood splattered the walls, fresh and still dripping. I felt the carpet squish under my shoes. Spinning around, I came face to face with a bed. Our bed.

Clare lay on the bed. The lips I'd kissed were spread open in a silent scream. Her eyes were open, but unseeing. She wouldn't even look at me. Even in death, she rejected me.

"I'm sorry."

I stumbled away.

Squish. Squish.

I ran.

My hands slapped against the wall as I stumbled.

It wasn't me.

"It wasn't me!"

Jerking upright, I stared at walls I did not recognize.

"I don't belong here. I'm not supposed to be here!" My voice echoed, boomeranging back at me, as the rain hammered down, confusing me even more. Where was I?

"I can explain. It wasn't me. I don't belong here. Let me out!"

Despite my cries, no one responded.

The bastards.

Maybe I just needed to kill them too.

26

Rain pounded down on the glass doors of the small health center. Ryker had driven the Prangers in his truck and followed her in. Still dripping, Rebecca stood with her arms hugging her body, staring into the parking lot.

The staff had assured her that it was hurricane-proof glass, like bulletproof glass. But Rebecca had seen enough instances of bullets tearing through things they weren't supposed to that she wasn't overly reassured by the comment.

The rest of the staff appeared to have felt the same way. They'd moved heavy furniture in front of the doors. Not enough to stop anyone from walking in if they needed, but enough to slow down anything that might manage to break through.

Though the structure was strong with a limited number of windows due to the nature of the business inside, everyone in the building had shifted to its center. They were all as far away from the hurricane as possible.

Except for Rebecca. She'd never seen a hurricane before, and Mother Nature's force entranced her. Earlier, she'd been out in it, too occupied to appreciate the awe-inspiring fury that Mother Nature could inflict so quickly.

Now I get storm chasers' fascination.

"Hey, Boss. You copy?"

Surprised to hear Hoyt's voice, Rebecca took the radio from her belt.

"I'm here, Hoyt. What's your location? Over."

"Uh. I'm not sure."

Ice ran through her veins, and she started looking around for her coat, sure she'd have to run out and search for her deputy.

"I know I'm close to the station, but not sure precisely where. Think you can turn on the exterior lights for me?"

Her shoulders unknotted slightly. "I'm not at HQ. Mr. Pranger needed to get checked out, so we all came to the health center. Locke is, though. Locke, you got your ears on? Over."

There was a long stretch of dead air.

While they waited on Locke, she reached out to her other deputy. "Darian, what's your status? Over."

"Wet. My status is very wet. Also, grumpy. With a strong chance of bitching. Over."

It felt good to laugh. But as tired and worried as she was, her laughter had a high chance of morphing into hysterical sobbing, so she cut it short.

"I do know I'm closer to you than I am to the station. All the cars managed to safely make it over the bridge, but I did one more sweep of homes. I think I'm only a couple blocks from you. I'm on Cove Drive, heading east. Over."

"Can you make it here? Over." She prayed his answer was yes because she didn't want him out in this craziness.

"I think so. Maybe. Ah hell, sir, I don't know. Everything has gone tits up out here, and I've got no visibility. The tires aren't holding either, and I keep sliding. The SUV isn't heavy enough to give me good traction. I'm currently just trying to stay between mailboxes. Over."

"Aim for the water that splashes, not the water with waves, Hudson. Over." Hoyt's joke fell flat.

"The wind's blowing so damn hard all the water has waves here in front of the town hall shelter." This came from Greg Abner. "Can someone tell me why the hell there are fish swimming through town? I'm about to flag down a dolphin and get a ride to Hawaii. Over."

Rebecca's smile was short-lived. She had two deputies out on the roads, lost, and it was less than an hour before the hurricane would be on top of them. Would shooting off a flare in this weather even be of any use? The wind was so strong it would send it off course immediately, but maybe they could see the light and estimate the direction?

It seemed like a terrible plan, but she couldn't think of any other way to signal to her men which way to go. Maybe if she had a lighthouse in her pocket, she could.

But if all she needed was light…

She stared at the spotlight she'd brought inside. Right before she was about to make a suggestion, another voice joined the channel.

"Hoyt, you there? Over."

"Ten-four, Locke, I'm here. Can you turn on the outside lights so I can find my way home? Over."

"Yeah, man. Not sure you'll be able to see them, but I can do that. Over."

"Hoyt, do your best to get to the station. But if you can't, then head for the shelter at town hall. I don't want you wasting any time on something that might put you in danger." Again, she looked at the heavy light. "Locke, are there any of the high-powered, handheld spotlights in the station? Over."

There was a short pause, then Hoyt's laugh came through.

"Shit. Of course there are. With the emergency road gear. Why didn't we think of that? Locke, you get to play human lighthouse. Over."

"Copy that. Great idea, Boss. Over."

Rebecca blinked as Locke called her *Boss* for the first time. Then again, maybe this was just another dig at her, and he had been referring to Hoyt. Either way, she didn't care so long as her people made it to safety.

Now it was time to see if she could implement her idea for Darian as well. Picturing in her mind his current location, she realized that he'd be coming directly toward the front of the center, which meant the lobby entrance was her best option.

She walked to the front doors and inspected the glass. It was clear these were double-paned with a gas barrier in between. Shining any light through them would not only bend but weaken the beam significantly, as each layer reflected the light inside.

That wasn't something she could risk with Darian starting so far away. The storm itself was going to add enough confusion. She had to get the doors out of the way of her light before it would work.

She examined the automatic system. As she feared, the doors were ancient, and she was unfamiliar with the mechanisms. She retreated to the nurse's station and found who she was looking for. Nurse Missy.

The nurse glanced up. "Need something?"

"Yes, you."

An eyebrow shot up. "For…?"

"I need to get outside to signal my deputy, but I'm not sure how to reactivate the automatic doors. Plus, it would be best if the doors closed behind me to keep the hurricane outside where it belongs. Can you help me?"

Nurse Missy popped to her feet. "And get away from charting? Absolutely."

As they jogged to the front entrance, Rebecca's radio crackled.

"Uh, Boss?" Darian's voice rumbled over the radio, the helplessness in it making her even more determined. "I don't suppose you've got one of those where you're at. Over."

She picked up her radio. "I sure do. That's what made me think of it. I'm working on a way to get outside where you can see me. And once I'm outside, I won't be able to use the radio and signal at the same time. And you wouldn't be able to hear me anyway. Over."

Hoyt laughed. "Put it under your raincoat! Over."

Nurse Missy flipped a switch on the control box for the inner doors, letting them part wide enough for Rebecca to step through into the atrium.

"Lost my last raincoat to Clarence." She mouthed a *thank you* as she squeezed past Nurse Missy. "He was freezing. The inside was covered in mud anyway. Besides, I can stand in the atrium after we get these doors open and swing the light for you to see. Over."

"Shit, sir, I don't even know how far away I am. Over."

"And I don't know if you'll be able to see this, but I'm going to try. Over."

She took several slow, deep breaths to brace herself for what was about to happen. The wind was already leaking through the outer doors, screaming to get in. Thinking that through, she told Missy to let the doors shut behind her. That would lessen the incoming wind, take some pressure off the door, and make sure gusts wouldn't rip through the lobby as soon as the outer doors were open.

"It's about to get loud, gentlemen. If you have something you want to say to me, say it now. Over."

Hoyt made one final joke. "Can you catch me a fish while you're out there? Over."

"Ha. It'll be a lot easier tomorrow once the water recedes. But then you'll need a trash bag instead of bait. Over."

Laughter rang out over the radio.

Staring into nature's rage knowing she was about to open herself up to it might qualify as clinically insane. Of course, that could only happen if she was strong enough to withstand the gale-force winds when they ripped through the open doors.

"Okay, Darian. Keep your eyes open. Here I go. Over." She set her radio down, out of the way of the wind and water.

She took another deep breath and turned to give Missy a thumbs-up. A few seconds later, the doors opened, and wind rushed in, slashing at her. Rebecca screwed her eyes closed and lowered her face, but the wind got more potent as it shrieked into the widening gap. She screamed with it as she strained not to get blown back into the inner doors.

The outer doors only opened a foot or so, just enough for her to squeeze through. Water poured in as wave after wave of rain sloshed over her. It was like standing in the surf.

Holding onto the door with one hand, she pulled the spotlight from her belt with the other. Ignoring the pain in her fingers as she squeezed the trigger, she raised the powerful beam toward the black canvas that enveloped the island.

The dark air lit up silver. She leaned back and tried to use the doors as a shelter. Her eyes followed the light as she waved it back and forth. Though she couldn't see it, she knew there was a road just on the other side of the parking lot. There was another one on the east side of the building. She tried to picture the map of the island in her mind, and the direction Darian would be coming from.

She kept her face down, trying to keep out of the water

spray so she could breathe. Wind sucked the air from her mouth while trying to replace it with bitter saltwater. It whipped so intensely that she had to use both aching hands to keep a grip on the light.

It was the most bizarre and intense workout she'd ever experienced. Fighting the wind and the rain, which switched directions erratically, she kept her movements slow and stable. Left, right, and left again, shining her light what she hoped was high enough for Darian to spot and low enough not to blind him. A slow burn of lactic acid buildup started in her arms, shoulders, back, and abdomen.

But she kept on swinging the light. Until the sound changed. The wind and sideways rain still roared, but there was something more. Something different.

Like a miracle, the cruiser slid to a stop in front of her. Rebecca cut the light and dropped her tired arms. Darian was out of the vehicle in a flash, a duffle bag slung over a shoulder. He fought the storm on his way in. He had to twist to the side and stretch as he shoved his bag through, then shimmied in. Once he was safely inside, the doors closed.

The noise was nearly unbearable as the wind pinched off and its pitch increased. Shaking her head, Rebecca bent to grab her radio. When the inner doors opened, they spilled into the lobby. The relative quiet was both a blessing and disconcerting at the same time.

"You two okay?" Nurse Missy's expression was filled with concern.

Rebecca wrung water from her hair. "Yeah. Thanks for your help."

After Missy seemed satisfied that they were indeed okay, she headed back to her station. "Hope you don't have to do that again," she called over her shoulder.

"Me too."

"So," Darian wiped the water from his face with both

hands and shook them off, "how do you like the weather in our little town?"

"It blows." Rebecca laughed and shook herself like a dog, making a mess of her hair, but she didn't care. "I think I prefer it when the ocean stays in the ocean."

"Ah, don't we all."

"I know I do." Ryker came around the corner at a trot. "Here ya go. When I saw Rebecca standing out there like that, I thought she might need one, and so would whoever she was signaling." He passed over two towels.

Edith Pranger stepped out as well and swatted at Ryker. "Oh, you. I'm the one who saw her and came to get you."

"I never said you weren't, ma'am."

"Here, dear, I asked around and managed to find some clean, dry clothes for you." Edith started to hand them over, then paused. "How about I just carry them for you? And your towel too."

Rebecca looked down at her dripping arms. The gloves on her hands had filled with water and drenched the gauze. This time, at least, her palms didn't sting with the thick layer of ointment the nurse had spread over them.

"I think that would be best. I'm not sure when I'm going to get dry clothes after tonight." She chuckled wryly. "I didn't board up my house or do anything else, or even call the owner. And I'm right on the eastern beach, so it's probably already blown out all the windows."

Darian flinched. "You didn't—"

"I've been working all night and haven't had a chance to go home," Rebecca cut in, not wanting to think about the mess that would likely be waiting for her. At least her safe was watertight.

"About that." Ryker smiled. "I swung by there this afternoon. All the windows are covered, and I stacked some bags in front of the doors. They don't work well for stacking, but

Quik-Brik will keep the water from getting in a house well enough."

Rebecca wasn't sure what those things were but was touched by the thoughtful actions. "You did that for me?" A thrill ran up from her toes when he blushed.

"Well. Yeah. That's what friends are for, right?"

Darian made a sound that started as a laugh but turned into a cough instead. He pounded his chest, his lips curving up at the corners. "Sorry, the cold must be getting to me."

"It's going to get to both of you if you stay in those wet clothes," Mrs. Pranger huffed.

"Come on in. Young man, we can find some dry clothes for you too."

"Thank you, ma'am." Darian referred to the bag on his shoulder. "My wife packed spare clothes for me, though. After all, what are friends for?"

Mrs. Pranger tittered a little laugh and reached out to take Rebecca's hand.

"C'mon, dear. Best to get cleaned up now, before the water heater goes out."

Rebecca let the older woman lead her away but couldn't stop thinking about that blush on Ryker's face. And how much of a ribbing she would get when she got back to the office.

27

The light flashed again, and Hoyt ducked his head. He knew where he was heading, but it nearly blinded him every time Locke swung the spotlight in his direction. He'd tried flashing his brights to signal he was close, but Locke must not have been able to see over the glare.

Hoyt had to deal with blue spots on his vision on top of the awful weather. He watched the light swing back around and ducked again to avoid the blinding. The light was coming from right beside him, so he knew he was close, but he still couldn't see the door.

"Screw it. Close enough." He put the cruiser in park. They would be leaving again soon anyway. It didn't matter if he was parked in the middle of the road. The vehicle would be just as likely to get hit by something no matter where it was. Pulling his hood up, he opened the door and dashed to the receding light.

It was only a few steps away. Locke had the light pressed on the door, and the whole thing was glowing. The younger man finally saw him and jerked out of the way.

Ripping the door open, Hoyt jumped inside.

"Damn, it's brutal out there. Is there any food left?"

Locke blinked but began stacking bags back against the door instead of answering.

Hoyt walked through the lobby. The half door was propped open, so he bolted for the breakroom. His stomach rumbled, but he wasn't sure if it was from hunger or pain.

Rebecca had been right. He was all messed up. Hunching over to avoid the worst of the wind and rain had made the cramps even worse. Hopefully, something warm in his stomach would ease his discomfort. For sure, he was dehydrated. He grabbed a cup and dipped it into the first slow cooker he reached.

He took a gulp, then gasped. "Ooh-hah. Oh, that's hot." Hoyt reached down and turned the setting from high to warm. "It's good, though." The broth was the perfect antidote for what currently ailed him.

"Uh, Hoyt?"

He took another sip before turning his gaze on Locke. The deputy appeared to be thoroughly freaked out. "What's wrong?"

"That dude in the back has been yelling for the last ten minutes now. That's why I couldn't answer the radio when you first called."

Shit. In all the excitement, Hoyt had nearly forgotten about their suspect. "Was he still in the interrogation room when you got here?"

"Yep. He was sitting at the table screaming his lungs out. I locked the door again but didn't enter." His eyes darted back and forth. "The man's lost it."

"He lost it last night. Now he's having to come to terms with that." Hoyt gulped some more food down. Now that his tongue was already scalded, it was easier. "Grab your shit. A go-bag, if you have one. And throw everything in the back of my cruiser." He tossed his keys over.

"We're leaving him here?"

"Hell no, man. Don't you know any SOP? We're taking him with us. He gets a police escort in handcuffs, but we got to get him out of this building before it falls down around our ears. Do you know how much paperwork we'll have to do if he dies while under our supervision?" Hoyt drained his cup and refilled it again, this time using the ladle he'd just spotted.

When he turned back, Locke was still standing there.

"What are you waiting for?"

"For you to tell me where you parked the Explorer. I couldn't see shit out there! You just popped up out of the fog."

Hoyt had to admit the kid had a point. They drove mostly tan cruisers, which blended in with the muck currently being thrown around. "Five running steps to the right of the door. In the street."

Locke spun on his heel and stomped off.

He could admit to himself that if he were a better man, he would apologize to Locke for snapping at him like that. Thankfully, he wasn't a better man, so he'd worry about that later. After all, Locke had never apologized to him for leaving his friend to die. Nor had he made any kind of amends to Rebecca for spreading the lie that it was her fault instead of his.

"Dammit." Hoyt slammed his empty cup on the counter and made his way back to the office before his morals could get a tighter hold on him.

He tried to open the door to the sheriff's office, but the knob didn't move. Of course Rebecca had locked it. That was where the evidence was. And she could follow the rules. The urge to make things better with Locke faded.

How many of these damn cases would have gone unsolved if Rebecca hadn't been here to deal with them?

How many more cases would have been swept under the rug or never brought to their attention? Would they even have connected the three cases involving the kidnapped little girls if they hadn't investigated the way she'd wanted?

All of that had been accomplished in spite of what Locke had tried to do. If people had believed him, she would have been let go. It was so hard to come to work with this man every day and not punch him in the face.

Today, it was even more challenging. Wallace had promised to make cocktails after the next hurricane. They'd planned to play some poker as a nod to the game of chance that their lives were. It was supposed to be a day to celebrate surviving another hurricane by playing cards while drinking with friends and coworkers.

Wallace always does things like that. Did. *He* did *things like that. He knew how to keep everyone together, even in the worst of times.*

Hoyt tucked that horrible feeling of loss away. It would be there waiting for him later, he knew. But right now, he couldn't deal with that. He pulled the key from his pocket and unlocked Rebecca's door. He was the only other person with a key to her office—though he couldn't open anything else inside. It was only the second time he'd had to use it in his career. The first one had been when Wallace locked up with his keys on his desk.

The boxes of evidence were no longer sitting there. Rebecca must have put them away in the locker, despite everything else that had happened that day. With that worry off his mind, Hoyt locked the office up again and went to check on their prisoner.

He could hear a steady thumping on the door as he got close. Opening the observation window, he couldn't see anything in the room.

"Move away from the door, Mr. Jenner."

The thumping stopped, and Malcolm's face popped up in front of the window, but he didn't appear to notice Hoyt watching him.

His face was twisted with grief. "Why are you holding me in here? I didn't do anything. I came to tell you what happened to Clare so you could help her." His fists slammed into the door, followed by his forehead. The hollow thump sounded again.

"Mr. Jenner, if you'd stop banging your head against the door, maybe we could talk."

"You have to let me out of here. I didn't do anything wrong. I'm innocent."

"Innocent of what, Mr. Jenner?"

There was a pause, and Jenner looked around, confused. "Innocent of whatever it is you think I did. I didn't hurt Clare. I found her like that. Then I tried to get help. Please, you have to help her. She didn't deserve that."

"Mr. Jenner, you're in there because you were a danger to yourself." Hoyt stepped to the end of the short hall and looked for Locke. He still wasn't back inside. What in the hell was taking him so long?

"To myself?" Malcolm's voice wobbled with fear.

"Yes, sir. You walked in here covered in blood. You didn't know your name. You could barely talk. Do you remember walking in here?"

"I...I remember a woman with dark eyes and a soft voice. She asked me something." He mumbled and spun around in circles, chewing at his thumb. "And I answered. I said...I said..."

"You said you thought you hurt someone." Hoyt watched as the man's face scrunched in confusion.

"Why would I say that?"

"I don't know. Why *did* you say that?"

"I can't remember."

"Well, after that, you didn't say anything at all. At least not anything that made sense. You were in shock. Do you remember being checked by the paramedics?"

"Paramedics? There was a light. I followed the light." He snapped his fingers. "An ambulance. I remember there was an ambulance. Did they get to Clare in time?"

There was so much hope in his eyes that Hoyt paused. The howl of the wind in the lobby let him know Locke was finally back. He darted toward the lobby and waved to catch his attention. Locke nodded and jogged his way.

"A lot has happened since then, Mr. Jenner. Do you remember the hurricane?"

"Hurricane? What hurricane?"

"Hurricane Boris. He's currently making landfall, and we're right in his path. We need to evacuate the building."

"But what about Clare?" Malcolm slammed his hand on the door. "Her house is close to the beach. She has to get to safety too. I can't leave without her."

Locke moved up beside Hoyt and gave him a nod. It turned Hoyt's stomach to only have Locke as his backup, but it was what it was. "We've already evacuated the rest of the island. It's too late for us to safely leave, but there's a shelter nearby. We're heading there."

Hoyt opened the door, and Malcolm's eyes darted up to his face, then down to the handcuffs he was holding. He backed away quickly, raising his hands defensively.

"Why the cuffs? I didn't do anything wrong."

As Locke stepped into the room, Malcolm raced around the table.

"It's to protect you and us." Hoyt held his hands up, soothing the man. "Do you remember how you got here? How you got those clothes? That blanket?"

For the first time, Malcolm seemed to take notice of his clothes. "These aren't mine. Where did they come from?"

"We gave them to you from our lost and found. You were soaked through, covered in blood and water, and you were in shock. Shock can do crazy things to people. That's why we need to cuff you. So you can't hurt yourself. Do you understand?"

"Hurt myself? I would never—"

"Are you really trying to tell me you don't have a headache from slamming your head into the door for the last ten minutes?" It was a bit of an exaggeration, but it got through to the man.

"I…don't remember."

"Exactly. So we need to cuff you and take you to the shelter. They have more resources, and we can ride out the hurricane there."

Like a prayer answered, the lights flickered, and the wind's screech increased. A loud metallic shriek started, making Hoyt wince. He hoped it wasn't one of their SUVs. Or the metal roof.

"Mr. Jenner, we need to get the hell out of here. Now." Locke stepped forward. "We can talk again once we're at the shelter."

"Okay. Yeah. Okay." Malcolm stopped dodging him and allowed himself to be handcuffed behind his back.

"Locke, grab the blanket and a coat. We need to get going now."

But when they reached the door and looked outside, Hoyt knew they were too late.

They'd have to ride the storm out at the station and hope for the best.

28

Wearing clean, dry clothes for the second time that day, Rebecca padded around in her hospital slippers. A sweet nurse had even brought her soap and shampoo and extra washcloths when she saw how much mud was caked into her hair and clothes. She had been given a room to work and sleep in. Lying in that bed had brought up a lot of bad memories, so she was up pacing instead.

Hoyt had contacted her to let her know they had Jenner, who was finally able to talk, and that they were sheltering in place at the station. She glanced at the clock on the wall again. The hurricane should be making landfall any minute.

Everyone else was glued to the radio, listening to the weather station. She'd already made her rounds. Clarence was safely tucked into a bed, snuggled up with Edith under three blankets. Darian was wearing a fresh, clean uniform and was sitting on a couch in the waiting area near the nurse's station. She had no idea if he was awake or asleep.

There was some talk that the hurricane would make land as a weak Category 3. It didn't matter to Rebecca. Not only did she not know the practical difference between categories, she knew it didn't matter.

Hurricanes could weaken or strengthen at any time. No one would know what had hit them until after it passed.

"Hey, Boss, you got your ears on? Over." Hoyt's voice came from the radio in her hand.

"Copy that. Over."

"We're using the back storeroom for shelter, and Jenner is starting to communicate. Over."

Rebecca frowned. "What does that mean? Over."

"It means he finally remembered that Clare is dead. Over."

Well, that certainly changed things for Malcolm Jenner, at least. He'd learned twice in one day that the love of his life had died. Rebecca could relate. Losing both her parents in the same night had turned her world upside down. The pain was a wound that could be torn open and exposed without warning. "You mean he didn't know before? Over."

"Nope. He kept asking if the ambulance had reached her in time. Over."

"Okay, something weird is going on here. Over."

Hoyt laughed into the radio. "Ya think? That's pretty par for the course, though, isn't it? Over."

"Well, yeah." She smirked and added, "But before, I could always blame it on politicians. Over."

"Ahh, you can keep blaming it on the politicians if you want. You're not going to hurt their feelings. They don't have any. Over."

That observation was so on the nose that she couldn't argue. "How did Jenner react when he realized she was dead? Over."

"That was weird too. He cried real tears. Even got kind of phlegmy. Then he told us we couldn't let Brady get away with this. Over."

"Brady? The dead woman's wounded husband? Over."

"That's the one. Over."

"What makes Jenner think Munroe did it? Over." She tried to think of where and how she had found Brady Munroe and wondered if it was possible. But if Munroe killed his wife, who attacked him? Could Clare have grabbed a knife before she retreated to her bathroom? If that were the case, why would she have come out of the bathroom, only to be attacked in the bedroom? Unless she attacked her husband first, in the kitchen, then they both went upstairs, and he finished her off.

But then, how did Jenner figure into all this? And how did he get so much blood on himself? And how did she end up the human equivalent of a mermaid?

"No clue yet, just theory. He was adamant we catch Brady Munroe, so maybe Jenner thinks Munroe killed Clare. Over."

It was time to get some answers. "Let's have a talk with Jenner and get all this cleared up now. Over."

"Uh, Boss? I'll just leave the mic on. He won't be able to hear you, but you can hear everything he and I say. Over."

"Ten-four. Over."

The latent sounds in the background got louder as Hoyt stopped talking. She listened to footsteps as he walked down the hall.

"We're going to see what he can tell us about what happened this morning. You ready?" Hoyt's voice echoed as he spoke.

"Ready as ever." That was Locke's voice.

Rebecca thought it was very telling that Hoyt made no mention of the fact that she was listening in. The silence through the radio was deafening, and she momentarily thought she lost the connection.

"Okay, Mr. Jenner, we're ready to listen now. Do I have your permission to record our conversation?"

"Yes." The word was so soft that Rebecca barely heard it.

Following normal protocol—even though their situation was far from normal—Hoyt stated the time and date as well as the people present. "Can you tell us what happened today? Start from the beginning."

There was a soft sob and a shaky sigh before Rebecca heard Malcolm Jenner's normal voice for the first time.

"Clare and I were supposed to meet up last night. Her husband was flying out of town on a red-eye, and she wanted company. We were going to have a little hurricane party and watch the storm over the ocean together. She said she had a new outfit to show me." He paused and let out a short huff of breath. Though his voice was laced with pain, he sounded clearheaded and sincere.

Hoyt stayed silent and let the man continue at his own pace.

"Clare loved mermaids, so I called her my little mermaid because she was always more graceful in the water than on land. We took a dance class together sometime last year, and she had two left feet. But she kept trying, and I learned how to dance in steel-toed boots. But then she took a water ballet class, and it was like a switch was flipped. She was so strong and poised, regal even. Like a mermaid. She loved it when I called her that. Thought it was magical."

For a few heartbeats, nothing else was said. His heartache and loss were evident, even through the radio. Rebecca pitied him until she thought about how the mermaid had ended up.

"What happened when you reached the island?" Hoyt prompted.

"I got to her house around two thirty in the morning. I wanted to make sure I got to the island before the bridge was closed. I had a spare key, so I let myself in."

"You had a spare key? How long had you and Mrs. Munroe been having an affair?"

She noticed he put emphasis on the *Mrs.*

Malcolm didn't seem to care. "A little over a year. Her husband was always gone. She said he had a girlfriend in every city he worked in. And that he didn't have time for her anymore. He didn't even care about her. They just lived together out of habit and convenience. It was rare they were even in town at the same time. She thought he'd planned it that way."

His voice rose, and his anger was clear, even though Rebecca couldn't see his face.

"He took her for granted. He'd come home with condoms in his luggage and expect her to put them away. It was like he wanted to rub it in her face. That he had all these women and she had no one. Until she had me."

"What happened when you opened the door?"

"Nothing at first. I called out to Clare, but she didn't answer. I heard a noise, though. When I followed the noise into the kitchen, Brady jumped me. He was covered in blood and had a knife in his hands. I fell back and hit the table. Somehow, we got turned around. I kept asking him what he'd done, but he wouldn't answer me. He was…his eyes…"

"What about his eyes?"

"He was crying. But he also looked like he wanted to kill me."

"How do you know he wanted to kill you?"

"Well, the damn knife was a good sign. And he kept screaming he was going to gut me. At first, I managed to fight him off because he didn't really seem like he was all there. He was thrusting the knife at me, but it was all over the place. Like I said, he wasn't all there. But then I slipped and fell on my back. He was on top of me, but I had ahold of his arm."

He paused to catch his breath.

"I grabbed his hand and got the knife away. And then I

tried to push him off. He got up, sitting on me, and moved to hit me, but I deflected it. I punched him. Just wanted to knock the wind out of him so I could push him off me." The pause was punctuated with a short sob.

"What happened next?"

"I punched him again with the hand holding the knife. I stabbed him in his side, I think. I must have. The knife disappeared after that. It didn't stop him, though. He kept trying to hit me. The whole time, I was screaming for Clare. I was so scared. There was so much blood on him. On his face and chest, on his arms. Then I realized he was bleeding too. He was bleeding on me. I guess he realized it, too, because he got up and ran off. Out the back door."

Jenner's voice had grown more ragged with every word, and Rebecca could hear him panting in reaction to his story. He was reliving those moments, which was something victims often did.

"And then what happened?"

"Then...then I got up. And I ran up to Clare's room. She still wasn't answering me. I opened the bedroom door. She was on the bed...covered in blood. I ran to her and tried to stop the bleeding. But she wasn't bleeding. She was just lying there, in the blood. Not moving. I tried to wake her up. I hugged her. I held her for...I don't know how long. Then there was something cold, and I really looked at her for the first time." He sobbed loudly and gasped for breath.

"What did you see?"

"He'd covered her in beach trash. Like he killed her, but that wasn't enough. It looked like he'd just scooped stuff up off the beach and smeared it all over her. I tried to clean her off. She shouldn't be seen like that. She was always so meticulous about her clothing, and especially her hair. That's when I knew I had to get help. So...I left her there. I left to get help."

When he didn't go on after a full minute, Hoyt prompted him again. "Where did you go?"

"I went out the front door because I'd left my phone in my car. But once I got outside, I don't know, I just started driving. The storm had intensified in the short time I'd been on the island, and a tree was down in the road. I didn't see it in time and slammed into it. I don't remember much after that. I was in the rain and felt lost. I didn't recognize where I was. And then…then I saw flashing lights, and I headed toward them." Malcolm sobbed brokenly.

There was a swish and the click of a door closing.

"You get all that, Boss? Over."

"I did. Over."

"He's done." Hoyt blew out a long, shaky breath. "He's curled up in a ball on the floor and crying his heart out. What do you think about it all? Over."

Rebecca had to think about that. "It matches every piece of evidence we currently have. All the parts have come together, and we're now seeing the facts through a new lens. Some science behind all our theories would be nice, though. Over."

"I gotta tell ya, Sheriff. You weren't sitting in there, but I believe him. At least, I believe he believes what he was saying. Over."

And that was the problem. Malcolm Jenner had had a mental break. He could have made up any kind of story in his mind. A story where he wasn't at fault for what happened.

"It could certainly be true. We won't know anything else until we can talk to Brady Munroe, and he hasn't woken up yet from surgery. Over."

"What do you want to do now? Over."

"The only thing we can do. Wait. And get some rest. Over."

"That sounds like a mighty fine plan to me. Hit me up if anything happens over there. Over."

"Same to you. Stay safe. I'll see you after this blows through. Over." Rebecca looked at the clock. It was time. There had been a steady building roar in the background for a while. The walls were thick, though, and the noise was ominous but tolerable.

The lights flickered off. Emergency lights came on immediately, bathing the room in a red glow. Pulling back the covers, Rebecca climbed into the bed. She was exhausted, and it was only half past three in the afternoon.

Whatever was going to happen was beyond her control now.

29

It was the quiet that woke her. Or maybe it was the change in the atmosphere.

Using the metal railing at her side, Rebecca pulled herself upright and looked around. She hadn't meant to fall asleep. When she'd climbed into the bed, she had intended to go through her notes on the case and stay alert in case anyone needed her.

Hopefully, she hadn't been needed because she didn't remember a thing after sitting on the bed. Rubbing her blurry eyes, she looked around the room and tried to take stock of everything.

She let out a relieved sigh until she glanced at the clock.

No!

That couldn't be right. Sitting up straight, she peered out the window. Blackness peered back. Slipping out of the bed, her slippers—like socks with a rubber grip pattern on the bottom—made no sound as she walked out into the hall.

Mostly silence greeted her, with a quiet murmur of people talking off in some public space. Rebecca moved toward the voices. It wasn't far, and two nurses' heads popped up as soon as she came into view.

"What time is it?"

Nurse Missy glanced at her watch. "Two twenty a.m."

The clock had been right after all. "You mean I slept through the entire thing?"

Nurse Missy grinned. "Well, not the entire thing, but the minute your head hit the pillow, you were out. I closed the door so you could sleep."

Rebecca rubbed her eyes. "I can't remember the last time I slept for eleven hours straight. Is everything okay?"

A tall nurse named Ryan smiled and nodded. "All the patients made it through the night without any real problems. So did the building. It got loud for a bit, but nothing broke. We haven't done rounds in the outer sections. Patients take priority. But everything seems peaceful."

"I'll do the rounds to check the building. Um, do you know, by any chance, what happened to my clothes? When I changed, I put them in a bag, and now I can't find it."

"If you put them in the cloth bag that was in the wardrobe, then laundry probably picked them up. We don't have enough generator power to run the machines, but we can toss them in as soon as we do."

Nurse Missy nodded at Rebecca's hands. "Let me check those."

Rebecca looked down at her hands as if seeing them for the first time. The bandages needed to be replaced, and the wounds needed cleaning, but she didn't have the heart to do that right then. "Rain check? I might end up getting them wet again doing rounds."

"Fair enough. Just don't go back to bed with them dirty, okay? Soiled bandages lead to infections."

"I'll make sure I stop in on my way back. Thanks." She waved and continued her walk. First, she wanted to check the entrances. Following the exit signs made them easy enough to find, but before she reached them, she found Darian.

He was sitting on a couch, his long legs stretched out in front of him and crossed at the ankles. His arms were folded over his chest. She was still ten feet away when his eyes snapped open, and his body tensed. His head whipped around. But when he saw her, he relaxed.

"Morning, Sheriff." His voice was hoarse.

"You know there's plenty of beds to choose from. You could have gotten a better night's sleep on one of those."

He laughed. "Are you kidding me? This is the most sleep I've gotten in a month. It's so nice and quiet here."

Remembering he had a newborn at home, Rebecca chuckled. "The hurricane isn't as loud, huh?"

"Doesn't even come close. Also, I don't care when the wind screams. My little girl, that's a different story." His smile wilted. "I would have slept better with her in my arms, though. Nothing more relaxing than a sleeping baby. With her little face and..." He scratched his stubble, clearly embarrassed.

It was an unexpectedly sweet side of Darian she'd never seen before, but it didn't surprise her.

"I can only imagine. And I put her at risk by not being available when the Select Board needed to take their vote on asking the governor for assistance." She waved her arm, indicating the entire building. "And all these people too."

"Nah, these people weren't ever going to leave. There are always some who refuse for one reason or another. You can't force them to be safe or smart." He shifted on the couch, then snorted. "Besides, you're not the one who gave us our marching orders. That was Greg. And he knew what he was doing. You did the right thing, not putting your nose in where it didn't belong."

He sighed, and his eyes got a faraway look in them. This wasn't the first time she'd seen him phase out like that. She'd heard it called a thousand-yard stare, and the name fit. Darian wasn't staring at the wall, though. He was firmly fixated on the past.

"You okay?"

"I've had plenty of commanders before who didn't have the balls to admit when they were in over their heads. And it ended poorly."

She didn't know what to say at first, then sighed, thinking about her own history. "Yeah, me too."

They shared a glance, then a nod. Then they both chuckled when they realized they were mirroring each other.

"Have you heard from all the guys?" Surely Darian would have told her if any of her deputies had been hurt, but she had to ask. "They okay?"

He dipped his head. "Everyone I know weathered the storm well."

Relief flooded through her. "That's good. Any more talk about that is going to require a couple of beers."

"More than a couple, I think."

"I drink big beers."

Darian rolled his eyes. "That's what they all say. And in case you're going to ask, don't worry about my girls. They left the island when I got called in. I'm not going to put them at risk for anything."

Yeah, she was going to ask about his wife and daughter. She was worried about every soul on Shadow Island. "That's good to hear. Are you up for a walk around? I want to see what the weather's doing and how much damage there is."

He stood, stamped his feet, and slung his bag over his shoulder. "Now's as good a time for a patrol as any."

She glanced down and noticed his military-issue combat boots. "If there's any broken glass, I'll let you deal with it."

He flexed his fingers. "Looks like I'll be doing the heavy lifting too."

She tucked her hands behind her back. "They aren't bad. Just keeping them wrapped to—"

"I saw how bad they were already. Remember? I'll do any lifting so they can begin to properly heal." A playful glint grew in his eyes. "Then you can do all the heavy lifting when they're scabbed over and itchy."

And with that tiny suggestion, her palms began to tingle.

When she rubbed them down her pant legs, he burst out laughing. "Power of suggestion is a real thing."

"Stop it! I'm trying not to think about how bad it's going to be."

"Want to talk about the mermaid case instead?"

Hell yeah.

"Talking about the case is the only thing I can do. It's not like I have anything to work on here. Who knows if our evidence survived? And I haven't even had a chance to talk with Brady Munroe yet."

She filled Darian in on Hoyt's discussion with Malcolm Jenner.

"That's weird. Trying to solve a murder in a hurricane isn't going to be easy. They're close to the beach, right? I hope the house held up. Otherwise, we've lost the crime scene too."

"They didn't take the hurricane seriously, so they didn't take any measures to secure the house. Hopefully, they still have a roof. Before we sheltered here, I saw a few houses that had already lost shingles. A tree fell in a yard, and Munroe and I barely managed to get out before it landed on us."

"You'll see even more once the sun is up. And roofs that are just missing."

They reached the barricade of furniture and stepped around it. Both sets of doors were still intact, but there was a puddle of water in the atrium between them. The tile floor inside was wet, but that could have been from people running in too. She'd left a big enough puddle on the floor herself.

Seeing that it was still secure, they turned right to follow the hall that wrapped around the exterior of the building. Rebecca stared out the windows. It was still raining, but it was a gentle rain. No leaves or debris being flung in its wake by strong winds. She was sure if she could see the ground or the surrounding buildings, it would be a different story, but what she saw from there was pristine.

"My mom always said that a good, hard rain cleaned the Earth. Not just the Earth herself, but all the people on it too."

"If that's true, then we're both clean as Heaven after yesterday."

Yesterday?

She couldn't believe that one day had already passed into the next.

Despite the horror and anxiety of yesterday, she had to admit she did feel clean. Or at least soothed and content. They walked in silence, taking two more right turns until they were back to where they'd started.

Everything was secure. No windows were broken. None of the other doors had leaked to an alarming degree. Even though the building was nearly half a century old, the builders had been smart to erect it high enough to avoid most storm surges.

All in all, they had escaped mostly unscathed by the terrible storm.

Then Rebecca's thoughts shifted back to the case at hand. "Not everyone deserves to be washed clean, though."

Darian caught onto her line of thinking. "Yeah, that would mean both Malcolm Jenner and Brady Munroe were clean too, and we both know they're not. Literally and figuratively. Seems like they were both covered in blood when they walked out into the rain."

His words triggered a memory.

"But all the blood didn't wash off them. Darian, you bagged Jenner's clothes. Did you happen to get pictures of them too?"

"Yeah, of course."

He flipped his bag around and dug out his camera. "Did you think of something? I have to admit, I didn't pay too much attention to it at the time. I was more focused on Jenner and the paramedics."

"I didn't see them at all. But I did think of something." She powered on the camera and started flipping through the pictures, zooming in on a few before moving on.

"Something interesting?" His curiosity was piqued.

Rebecca flipped back and forth between several pictures, frowning. "Always something interesting when you look at the evidence. What seemed like nothing before can take on a different meaning as you gather more pieces of the puzzle. Everything tells a story if you put it in the right order."

"What story does his clothing tell you?"

"That I'm missing a larger portion of the whole story. I wonder if there's a printer I can use."

30

The sound of people talking woke Rebecca, and she jerked upright, slamming her back into the chair as she looked around the room. It took her a few breaths to understand where she was, what had happened, and why she was waking up in a chair in the middle of a medical room.

After getting the pictures printed at a station powered by the generator, she'd finally submitted to getting her wounds cleaned. It had been nearly four when she'd returned to her room and settled down in the chair, using a rolling table for a desk. The images she'd gone through had indeed told a whole different story than what she'd imagined.

But even the new information hadn't been enough to keep her awake for long.

A glance at the clock told her it was nearly six in the morning.

"Sheriff West?" Someone knocked on her door, even though she'd left it ajar.

"Yes?" She pulled herself up in her chair and tried to brush her hair back while flipping the pictures over. No one else needed to look at what she'd uncovered.

The door swung open, and a woman in scrubs without a name tag held up a bag. "I heard we picked up your clothing by mistake. Most of our machines run on the main power, but we have one set that's hooked up to the generator. Thought you might need these, so I took care of them for you."

Something in the elderly woman's smile made Rebecca do a double take as she got up to retrieve her items. "Thank you so much for going through the trouble. I appreciate it."

As soon as the woman was gone, she dumped the bag out and inspected everything. Her belt was there, along with all her tools. Even her thick gloves were there. She went over everything with a fine-tooth comb.

When she pulled out her badge, her heart warmed.

She wasn't the only one who had gone over her things meticulously. Everything she'd been wearing yesterday had been splattered, smeared, soaked, and drenched in blood, rain, and mud. Now, it was all pristine—literally down to her shoes and the laces in them.

A loop of black in the bottom of the bag caught her eye. Reaching in, she knew what it was as soon as her fingers touched it. The black hair tie she'd used to keep her hair back had been crusted in mud when she'd struggled to get it out of her hair in the shower last night.

Now, like everything else, it was clean and ready to be used again. Even her badge had been polished. And she knew there was no way she'd put either of those things in her bag.

Someone had come in and taken care of her. Now all she needed was a hairbrush and a cup of coffee, and she'd be ready to face whatever the day threw at her.

It was more than a little disconcerting, but she appreciated the effort.

Feeling better than she'd thought possible, she opened the door to the bathroom and stepped in to wash her face.

Next to the sink was a disposable hairbrush and toothbrush.

"And I want to win the lottery today too." Rebecca figured she might as well push her luck a little more.

With her hair brushed and pulled back neatly, back in her own clothes and shoes, she headed out to see if she could scrounge up a cup of coffee before getting to work.

Dr. Evan was standing at the nurses' station and looked up as she approached. "Looks like someone had a good night's sleep."

"I did. And your staff was kind enough to collect my mud-soaked things and wash them for me."

Dr. Evan laughed. "That's the kind of thing we do for heroes around here."

"I'm no—"

"Save it." The doctor shook her head. "If you hadn't found Brady Munroe when you did, he would have died. Even without the hurricane."

"Is he still being guarded?"

Dr. Evans inclined her head. "Like a hawk. By the way, here are his personal effects. I know you're going to need them."

She slid a stack of clear plastic bags over. Rebecca spread them out like a deck of cards. The shirt caught her attention immediately.

"She also saved Clarence yesterday." Nurse Missy smiled at Rebecca with stars in her eyes that made her uncomfortable.

Rebecca shook her head and picked up the bag to get a better look. "That was Ryker Sawyer."

"I heard she had to get Walter off his roof too. Like a scared cat that refuses to jump."

Rebecca frowned and manipulated the bag to shift the fabric around inside it. When hospital staff bagged clothes, they didn't bother to lay them flat or anything. She had to straighten out the shirt inside to see if she was seeing what she thought she was seeing. "That was Deputy Hoyt. I just pulled the rope to extend the ladder."

Dr. Evan huffed and turned to Rebecca with her fist on one hip. "Which was so difficult to do, it shredded both your hands. I don't see Deputy Hoyt in here needing medical attention after that rescue."

"He should be, but he's stuck at the station. I'll make sure he has time to come in for a checkup today. Or a follow-up with his doctor, at least." Rebecca was too intrigued by what she saw to pay much attention. Setting the bag aside, she picked up the one that held Munroe's pants. Then looked for his personal effects. It contained his wallet and a watch but no keys.

"He didn't have his house keys on him."

"Sheriff?"

Rebecca looked up to see the doctor frowning at her.

"Did you find something important?"

She chewed on her inner cheek for a moment as she thought things through. "Can you tell me the nature and location of Brady Munroe's wounds?" Saying wounds, plural, was a guess, but it paid off.

"He had a large laceration in his side. Nicked his liver. He would have bled out if he'd not been found. And several wounds on his hands." Dr. Evan looked at the clothes, then back up at Rebecca. Her brows slammed together. "Wait. Didn't I hear that his attacker didn't have any wounds?" She pulled the bloody shirt in the bag out and stared down at it.

"Yes." Rebecca nodded. "Can you compare his blood to the blood we took from Clare's chest?"

"Not without his consent or a warrant."

"Then take the blood from the coat he was wrapped in when he came in." She found the bag with the coat and flipped it over to show *Sheriff* written across the back of it. "That's my personal possession and doesn't affect his bodily autonomy."

"I can do that. But we can't do more than a blood type match here."

"What are we matching?" Darian stepped up behind Rebecca.

It made her jump.

"Woah there, Boss. Maybe you don't need this java after all."

He held a large cup of coffee, and she reached for it. Wisely, Darian did not fight her for it.

"Have we gotten a statement from Brady Munroe yet?"

He shook his head. "I haven't. He was still out cold and recovering, last I heard."

"He's awake now. And lucid. I just came from checking on him." Dr. Evan slid the bag back to Rebecca and frowned. "I see what you're talking about. And you should definitely go have a talk with him. I'm sorry."

Rebecca saw the understanding in her eyes. She had seen the same thing Rebecca had and put the pieces together in the same way. "I'm not. I may not have saved a victim, but I did save an innocent man from going to jail."

31

Rebecca waited while Darian rapped his knuckles on Brady Munroe's door. She'd already explained the conclusion she'd come to after seeing the evidence, and he agreed with her. Before Munroe responded, Darian swung the door open in a commanding way.

Rebecca stepped around him, carrying a pad of paper and a pen. She'd learned long ago that taking notes made a suspect forget about being recorded. She hoped it would work this time too.

Munroe struggled to wiggle his way up in the bed, wincing as he twisted.

"Hello, Mr. Munroe. I'm Sheriff West. Do you remember me?"

He frowned and shook his head. "No, I'm sorry. Have we met before?"

"Not before yesterday. I was the one who found you and brought you in. You were on the beach."

His gaze moved down her body. "You're the one who saved me?"

She smiled, resisting the urge to reach for a handful of

sanitizer gel. "Yes, sir. And I'm thrilled to see you doing so well."

"Because of you, young lady. I owe you my life. Literally."

She forced her gaze to slip down to his lips before meeting his eyes again. "It was my pleasure."

Though it disgusted her to do it, a law enforcement officer was allowed to use every tool in their arsenal to get a confession. They could lie, exaggerate, even flirt. Which made sense, because an interrogation was more like a seduction instead of the coercion TV cops made it appear to be.

"Well, thank you all the same."

Lifting her phone, she mentally crossed her fingers. Though Virginia was a one-party consent state, and Munroe wasn't officially under arrest, she'd feel better getting proper consent to record the proceedings. If she nailed this guy, she didn't want a defense attorney tossing the confession on a technicality.

She tapped record on her phone and set it on the bedside table away from his line of sight. "Mr. Munroe, do I have permission to record our interview today?"

He started to smile but seemed to catch himself and frowned instead. "Of course. I want to do anything I can to help you find the monster who killed my wife."

She practically simpered her thanks. "That's very kind of you. Mr. Munroe, can you tell us the events that led up to me finding you unconscious in your backyard?"

"I'd gone to the airport for a business trip, but the flight was canceled, so I returned home." He inhaled a long breath and winced, moving a hand over his side. "When I got home, there was a man standing over my wife in our bedroom. She was already dead. Then he attacked me too. I barely managed to get away from him. I don't know where he went after that."

Tears spilled down his cheeks. His bottom lip quivered.

Wow. Is he in sales? That would make sense, because he's really selling this act.

It was too bad for him that she'd already compared the physical evidence. And based on her theory, it was virtually impossible for Malcolm Jenner to have killed Clare. The pieces of the puzzle all pointed to Munroe. She just needed a confession.

Already prepared for his deception, Rebecca held up a printout. "Is this the man you saw?"

Munroe made a little show of looking startled before morphing into rage. It was an exceptionally good act—the wounded, grief-stricken husband—but still willing to talk in order to catch his wife's murderer. And in a twisted way, that was precisely what he was doing.

"His name is Malcolm Jenner. We believe Clare was having an affair with him, and that's why he was at your home yesterday."

"No." His lips clenched, and he shook his head, wiping his face with the gauze on his right hand. "My wife would never cheat on me. Never. She loved me. We were devoted to each other. Our lives together were nearly perfect. There's no way she would risk that for some weakling like him."

"What makes you think he's weak?"

Munroe snorted so hard he gripped his side again. "Come on, now. Look at that guy and look at me. I've got at least thirty pounds on him, all muscle. I go to the gym every day. He looks like he spends his life behind a desk. Why would she ever go for a guy like him when she's got a man like me in her bed?"

Rebecca couldn't stop the moue of disgust at his words, but he was narcissistic enough to take it as a good thing.

"See? Exactly." He pointed at her mouth. "Even you can't help but be disgusted by the idea."

"But if you're so much stronger than him, how did he manage to wound you?" she asked innocently.

He scowled. "Because I was in shock. Obviously. I was staring at my dead wife, covered in blood. And he's standing there like a lunatic. Leaning over her. Smiling. I never even saw the knife in his hand before he attacked me with it."

"Did it look like Clare fought back at all?"

"What do you mean?"

"Did he have scratches on his face? Torn clothing? Or do you think he surprised Clare the same way he surprised you?"

Rebecca watched him weigh those options. She'd bet her truck he was thinking of the lie that would make him look best. Make him look strong and masculine, and all those other gross things that men like him worried about. At the same time, he would want to make the other man look weak and small.

His response would dictate how she continued her line of questioning.

"No. He didn't have a mark on him. He was probably hiding in the shadows, a thin guy like him and a madman to boot, and my poor wife didn't even know he was there. If I hadn't come in when I had, he would have gotten away scot-free." He covered his face with his hands. "My poor wife. It was so awful. She was covered in blood, desecrated, and defiled, while he stood there looking like he'd just come from a debate meeting. Then, he sucker punched me."

The son of a bitch hasn't even said her name once.

"Her name was Clare," Darian's voice grated out.

Rebecca darted a glance over to her deputy, not surprised that he'd also caught on. She signaled him to stay quiet, then noticed the change in Munroe. He puffed up, going into combat mode against the beefed-up, handsome, younger man.

I can use this.

Darian stood with his arms loose, but his shoulders were tight, and his stance was wide. He was fighting mad. She gave him a subtle nod to encourage him to piss the man off further. Maybe that was the fastest way to break a narcissist like Munroe—get him angry and defensive.

"What?"

Darian took a step closer. Not close enough to hover over the man, but enough to threaten his masculinity. "Your wife. Her *name* was Clare."

Munroe's face screwed up in disgust and anger. "I know my wife's name. I don't need you to remind me of it."

"Then why haven't you said it?"

"What?"

Rebecca wiggled her fingers, motioning for Darian to keep egging him on.

"I'll speak slower so you can understand. The entire time you've been telling us this little story, you've never once said Clare's name. You've only referred to her by her relationship with you. Not as her own person."

Munroe's mouth popped open. "I loved my wife."

"Clare." Darian's nostrils flared. "Are you not saying Clare's name because you feel guilty for killing her? Or are you not saying her name because you never saw her as a person in her own right?"

"How dare you say that to me? She was my wife, and I loved her!" Brady glared at Darian but sat there calmly enough.

Darian took a step closer. "But did you love her like a person or like an acquisition?"

"What kind of question is that? I loved her like my wife!"

The sad thing was, he really did seem confused by that. He couldn't understand the difference between loving a woman and loving a new car.

"Did you let Clare know that your flight had been canceled, Mr. Munroe?" Rebecca asked.

Munroe did a double take, confusion marring his features. "Huh?"

"Did you call Clare to let her know that your flight had been canceled?"

Rebecca asked the question for two reasons. One was to keep him on his toes, going back and forth between her and Darian. The second was because it would be easy to follow up on his answer.

He searched her face for a full minute before answering. "No. I decided to surprise her."

She smiled, as if that were the most romantic thing she'd ever heard. "That's so nice of you."

Munroe shot a superior glance at Darian. "That's just the type of husband I am."

Rebecca forced the smile to morph into sadness. "But something terrible went wrong when you got home, didn't it?"

He mirrored her expression. "Yes. It was terrible."

"You found her preparing for a visit from another man."

"Ye—" He shook his head. "No. What are you talking about?"

"It's okay, Mr. Munroe." Sympathy oozed from her voice. "I understand. You planned to surprise her, and there she was, betraying you."

He stared at her. "She wouldn't do that." Even now, he refused to believe that his wife would want someone else.

Keeping her voice soft and filled with gentle kindness, Rebecca leaned closer to him. "I can't even begin to understand how terrible it would have been for you to find her dressing up to be with another man. It must have been a terrible fight."

"I—" He clamped his mouth closed.

"But you showed her, didn't you? After the fight, you went downstairs and got a knife. I bet you just wanted to scare her at first. What did she say that finally forced you to stab her?"

Yeah, it's all her fault. Tell me all about it.

Another full minute passed, and Munroe began to sweat. "That's not how it happened."

"When she was dead, you needed to teach her another lesson, didn't you? Is that why you decorated her like the horror movie version of a mermaid? Was that to mock what she was going to share with Jenner?"

"Or did you just feel guilty for killing the woman who trusted you with her heart?" Darian added. "A heart that you put a knife through."

Munroe's nostrils flared. "I told you what happened!" Spittle flew from his mouth.

"But what you say happened doesn't fit with our evidence, Mr. Munroe." Rebecca waited until she had his full attention again. "You see, we know you arrived at your house before Jenner. We know you had a fight with Clare and that you stabbed her. After stabbing her, you put on a rain slicker to go outside and collect seaweed and shells to decorate her with."

A rivulet of sweat trickled down Munroe's temple. "No. I wouldn't."

Rebecca brought her sympathetic expression back. "But you did. You see, when you put the rain slicker on, it protected your shirt from the weather. It also kept Clare's blood spray from washing away. I believe you were going back outside when Jenner arrived. You two fought in the kitchen, which was when you were stabbed. You ran outside and collapsed where I found you."

The muscle in Munroe's jaw worked. "I don't know what you're talking about."

"Jenner, uninjured, went upstairs to check on Clare. After finding her, he left out the front door to find help and came to the sheriff's station."

"You're lying. There's no way you can prove any of that. There's nothing to say things didn't happen precisely the way I said they did. And if that's what that madman told you, then he's lying." He held his arms out. "Look at me. If I attacked Jenner, if I was the madman, then why isn't he dead? If it were a fair fight, I would've won."

"Maybe. But it wasn't really a fair fight, was it?"

He snorted. "What are you talking about?"

"Your hands." She held up her own gauze-wrapped fingers.

He twisted his hands under the blanket, trying to hide them from her knowing gaze.

"It's a real bitch trying to hold onto anything when your hands are already sliced up, isn't it?" She glanced up at Darian.

Darian nodded. "Knife handles get real slick once they're covered in blood. Especially ones like kitchen knives with smooth-grain wood. That's why combat knives have grooves or wrapping on them. And a guard before the blade. Otherwise, the hand slides down and onto the sharp edge, cutting the user."

Rebecca jumped back in. "By the time Jenner showed up, your hands were already cut from killing Clare, swollen from digging in the sand, punctured from wrapping the barbed wire around her legs, and stiff as hell from all of the above. You couldn't hold onto the knife you attacked him with. Your arms were tired from stabbing Clare so many times and with so much force that the knife pierced through her body in places and cut the mattress underneath her. Jenner was able to fight you off because of that, take the knife out of your hand, and stab you, even though you were on top of him."

Darian made a *tsk* sound. "Then you ran away while he went to check on the woman you claim to love so much. And he held her on that bed."

Rebecca enjoyed the way the man's head whipped from side to side as they took turns nailing him with their evidence. "Deny it all you want. But the blood told me everything I needed to know. On your clothes, there are active splatters. They're all focused mainly on your shirt. On your chest, neck, and sleeves. From where you plunged the knife in, then raised it overhead. But on Mr. Jenner..." She shook her head. "The blood on his clothes was on his stomach and legs in wide, concentric circles. That shows the blood soaked into his clothing as he held her in his lap, trying to save her."

Munroe's mouth twisted, and he crossed his arms over his chest. He wasn't asking for a lawyer, but she knew that was coming. The only thing standing between him and a defense attorney was arrogance.

"We took samples from the blood on Clare's chest. Where your cut hands bled on her chest after you twisted the knife into her heart."

His bottom lip actually popped out a little. "That's not true."

"Yes, it is. You attacked *your wife*, and Malcolm Jenner tried to protect her, as a real man would."

With a cry of rage, Munroe lunged at Rebecca.

Darian darted forward, grabbing Munroe's shoulder and pressing him back into the bed. His arm was handcuffed to the railing a second later.

"She was my wife. My wife! My mermaid. Not his. She only dressed up like a mermaid for me, not him! She had no right to do that in my home! Where the neighbors could see."

Softening back into her good cop role, Rebecca slid back into sympathy. "When you saw her dressing up like a mermaid for another man, you couldn't allow that, could you? You had to kill her. You had no other choice."

He leapt on the word. "That's right. She didn't give me a choice. And even after all she'd done to me, I still gave her what she wanted. I made her up like a mermaid, and I was going to release her to the sea so she could live out the rest of her life on her own."

Rebecca shivered. If not for a hurricane, Munroe might have gotten away with his crime. Disgusted to her core, she stepped away from the bed and nodded for Darian to take over. As she walked from the room, she heard the most beautiful words in the world.

"Brady Munroe...you're under arrest for the murder of Clare Munroe..."

32

Diminishing winds blew through town as Rebecca drove her cruiser home. After everything that had happened, she just wanted to see her little rental and rest for a bit. Storm debris fluttered in every yard and ran down the gutters of town. But the winds also broke up the clouds, and the blue sky peeked through.

Cars dotted the streets as people returned to their homes, anxious to see what damage there was or if they'd been among the lucky ones whose homes made it through unscathed. Plywood was everywhere. It covered windows, hanging at angles where it hadn't been secured well enough, or flapping on rooftops where shingles had been stripped off.

When she reached her rental, her shoulders slumped in a mixture of disbelief and awe. While her neighbor's cottage was destroyed completely, the little cottage she loved so much was still standing.

Why theirs and not hers?

Shadow's force of nature didn't make sense.

Her rental wasn't completely unscathed. Shingles were

missing, as well as long strips of siding. The plywood that Ryker had put in place had protected the windows, though, and the structure appeared to be sound.

On the outside, at least.

Parking in the driveway, she climbed out, took a deep breath, and instantly regretted it. The thing about storms from the ocean was they always deposited deep-sea plants and animals on the beach. Then scavengers would swarm over them as they decomposed faster in the sun.

Hopefully, there wouldn't be anything like that in her backyard. Wishing she had a shovel just in case, Rebecca walked around the house. The patio had uprooted patches of grass plastered all over it but was, thankfully, free of anything else.

A quick inspection showed that the panels over the back door that protected the glass were flush with the trim. There wasn't even a gap for her to see through, so she knew there was no chance it had broken in the storm. Rectangular lumps of poorly cured concrete lay along the bottom of the barricade. She figured they must be the bricks Ryker had told her about.

While her house was perched on stilts, as were almost all the beach homes on the island, there were signs that the water had risen high enough to lap at the base of the bags. Maybe the inside was okay, after all.

Resting her hands on her hips, she smiled as she took in everything. Her little getaway might look like a barren fortress right now, but she was assured that it was mostly intact. All she had to worry about was informing the homeowner of the damage to the roof and siding.

Her stomach dropped as she realized something important. Her back deck was completely empty.

"Shit. The patio furniture!"

Turning in a circle, she tried to find her missing items in the neighboring yards. There was no sign of them. The chairs would have traveled much farther than the heavier table, so if she couldn't find the table, there was no way she was going to spot the chairs. They could be in D.C. by now.

"Looking for something?" a voice called out.

She spun around, and Ryker was leaning out his truck window, waving. He looked even more tired than she felt.

She rubbed her eyes. Were the legs of her furniture sticking up from the truck bed?

"Your door was locked yesterday, so I couldn't put them inside. I took them home with me instead. Sorry, I forgot to tell you that. Thought I'd beat you home today. I didn't mean to make you worry."

Rebecca didn't miss the way he ducked his head after talking. She knew that meant he was feeling self-conscious and worried. It was incredibly endearing. He parked along the curb, and she jogged over to meet him. She reached his door just as he closed and leaned against it.

"Thank you so much. I didn't even have time to think about it yesterday."

He ducked his head again. "That's the same reason I forgot to tell you. There was a lot going on. Don't even worry about it." He reached out for her hand but changed the gesture to point at the bandages instead. "How about you grab the chairs while I carry the table up?"

She tried to assure him. "They're really not that bad. Mostly healed, in fact."

He shrugged her off. Which was too bad because she wouldn't mind a bit of holding hands right then.

"Table's not really heavy enough to need two people to unload it anyway." He turned and, using the tire, stepped up into the bed and handed down the chairs. She picked them up as he lifted the table out and set it on the ground.

"I owe you for everything you did yesterday." Rebecca wanted to repay him with a meal and almost offered, but her crazy schedule made her hesitate a bit too long.

"You don't owe me anything. I'm under contract with the owner. It's my job to keep the house maintained."

"Well, I owe you one clean t-shirt."

Her bold comment seemed to render *him* speechless for a change.

"Well, it looks like I'll need to come by and check the roof. You're missing a lot of shingles up there. I can grab it then." A hint of red started at Ryker's neck, just above his collar. He picked up a work belt and cinched it around his hips.

She shifted her attention away from him and peered at the roof as well. "Yeah. I haven't been inside yet, so I don't know if it leaked or not. Those boards are on too tight to pull off without a tool of some kind."

He hopped off his truck, picked up the table, and started walking to the back deck. She followed him with a chair under each arm. "I've got tools in my truck to take those down. Don't worry. I'll get it all set straight again." The corners of his lips pulled up in a half smile. "Besides, I owe you for helping me find Clarence yesterday."

She grinned. "Just doing my job. Keeping our community and neighbors safe."

With a gentle *thunk*, he set the table down in its place.

"I like the sound of that."

She tilted her chin to the side and arranged the chairs as she watched the smile stretch his lips. "What? Keeping things safe?"

He shook his head. "Hearing you say *our* community. It sounds like you're thinking of making things permanent."

"I…" Heat filled Rebecca's cheeks, and she had no idea what to say. It was true. This place—not just this house, but this island—was starting to feel like home. Home in a way she hadn't felt for years now. "I guess you're right."

Ryker pulled a hammer from his belt and spun it in his hands. "How about we get you inside then? And we can see if there's anything wet that needs to be dealt with."

The double entendre made the blush in her cheeks flare, and she was, once again, left unable to find any words.

His jaw dropped, and he held up his hands. "I did not mean it like that. I meant that we needed to check the roof for leaks or standing water." He spun around to face the plywood. "Oh, look, a job that needs to be done. Let me just get to that."

Before Rebecca could come up with a response, her phone rang. It was in her hand before she even had a chance to think. The display showed a call from the station, and she groaned.

Wishing she could pretend her phone still didn't have service but knowing her professionalism wouldn't allow it, she answered the call.

"This is West."

"Hey, West, I'm back!" Viviane's voice was as bright and cheerful as always, and Rebecca gave a quiet sigh of relief.

"I'm so happy to hear that. Have you been by your place yet? Is everything okay?"

"Yep, but I can tell you all about that later. Right now, Hoyt needs you down at the beach."

Worry niggled at Rebecca's nerves, and she remembered she'd meant to tell her senior deputy to get checked out by his doctor before coming in for his next shift. "Did something happen?"

"You could say that. The hurricane washed two bodies up on the beach."

The End

To be continued...

Thank you for reading.

All of the *Shadow Island Series* books can be found on Amazon.

ACKNOWLEDGMENTS

How does one properly thank everyone involved in taking a dream and making it a reality? Here goes.

In addition to our families, whose unending support provided the foundation for us to find the time and energy to put these thoughts on paper, we want to thank the editors who polished our words and made them shine.

Many thanks to our publisher for risking taking on two newbies and giving us the confidence to become bona fide authors.

More than anyone, we want to thank you, our readers, for sharing your most important asset, your time, with this book. We hope with all our hearts we made it worthwhile.

Much love,

Mary & Lori

ABOUT THE AUTHOR

Mary Stone

Mary Stone lives among the majestic Blue Ridge Mountains of East Tennessee with her two dogs, four cats, a couple of energetic boys, and a very patient husband.

As a young girl, she would go to bed every night, wondering what type of creature might be lurking underneath. It wasn't until she was older that she learned that the creatures she needed to most fear were human.

Today, she creates vivid stories with courageous, strong heroines and dastardly villains. She invites you to enter her world of serial killers, FBI agents but never damsels in distress. Her female characters can handle themselves, going toe-to-toe with any male character, protagonist or antagonist.

Discover more about Mary Stone on her website.
www.authormarystone.com

Lori Rhodes

As a tiny girl, from the moment Lori Rhodes first dipped her toe into the surf on a barrier island of Virginia, she was in love. When she grew up and learned all the deep, dark secrets and horrible acts people could commit against each other, she couldn't stop the stories from coming out of the other end of her pen. Somehow, her magical island and the darkness got mixed together and ended up in her first novel. Now, she spends her days making sure the guests at her beach rental cottages are happy, and her nights dreaming up the characters who love her island as much as she does.

Connect with Mary Online

facebook.com/authormarystone
twitter.com/MaryStoneAuthor
goodreads.com/AuthorMaryStone
bookbub.com/profile/3378576590
pinterest.com/MaryStoneAuthor
instagram.com/marystoneauthor
tiktok.com/@authormarystone

Made in the USA
Las Vegas, NV
05 September 2024